D1445972

THE ADULTERESS

THE ADULTERESS

LESLIE MARGOLIN

FIVE STAR

An imprint of Thomson Gale, a part of The Thomson Corporation

THOMSON

GALE

Detroit • New York • San Francisco • New Haven, Conn. • Waterville, Maine • London

THOMSON
— ★ — ™
GALE

LIBRARY OF CONGRESS CATALOGING-IN-PUBLICATION DATA

Margolin, Leslie, 1945–
   The adulteress / Leslie Margolin.—1st ed.
      p. cm.
   ISBN 1-59414-481-8 (hardcover : alk. paper)
   1. Rattenbury, Alma Victoria—Fiction. 2. Stoner, George Percy, 1916–
—Fiction. 3. Rattenbury, Francis Mawson, 1867–1935—Fiction. 4. Adultery—England—Fiction. 5. Murder—England—Fiction. 6. Husbands—Crimes against—Fiction. I. Title.
PS3613.A74A65 2006
813'.54—dc22   2006013948

U.S. Hardcover:
ISBN 13: 978-1-59414-481-3
ISBN 10: 1-59414-481-8

First Edition. First Printing: December 2006.

Published in 2006 in conjunction with Tekno Books and Ed Gorman.

Printed in the United States of America on permanent paper
10 9 8 7 6 5 4 3 2 1

This novel was inspired by the facts of a well-known case, but the characters attributed to the individuals represented are based on the author's imagination, and are not necessarily factual.

To Mom, with love and thanks

And I will judge thee as women that break wedlock and shed blood are judged, and I will give thee blood in fury and jealousy.

—Ezekial

1

Felix, my six-year-old son, was beside me when I crashed the Daimler into a basement shop window. The impact knocked me unconscious. His wailing woke me. I don't understand anatomy; I can't give you a medical explanation for the injury, but the doctors said there was some question whether he'd walk again. The shameful part is that I should not have been window-shopping while driving. Felix could have been killed and it would have been my fault if he had.

I promised my husband Rats to never drive again. He would do all the driving from now on. But the third morning after the accident, when I asked him to drive me to visit Felix at his hospital in Dorchester, he refused. "Come on, Alma," he said, "you'll be making him into a sissy."

Rats wasn't a monster. He wasn't even a bad man. But he had a highly developed awareness of masculine duty, and he was rather slow to grasp a point, a combination that made it nearly impossible for him to show tenderness toward his son, and necessary for me to pound the walls and scream in order to get him to agree to drive me. Not a felicitous way to resolve a disagreement, but neither was it unexpected. You could say that it represented a new low in our relationship but you could also say our relationship had always been declining.

I was twenty-eight when we met. This was in Victoria, Canada, in April 1924. My employer, who had gone to Oxford with him, was giving a party to celebrate the completion of the

Empress Hotel, which Rats designed. I could see that he was delighted over the fuss everyone was making of him. He was surrounded by admirers, jammed into a corner between the piano and the bar, close enough to the bar that he could refill his glass without taking a break from conversation. He was, I would come to see, the type of borderline alcoholic whose salvation seems to lie in continuous displays of affection: everybody acting as if they adore him, and he acting as if he adores everybody. He was the misty-eyed hero of the party and I was only a secretary, but from the way he was glancing in my direction, I could tell he'd noticed me.

And I was right. "How do you do?" he said bowing slightly, holding out a hand that was really bigger than my whole head. "Francis Rattenbury. I hope I'm not disturbing you."

"Not at all," I said smiling sweetly. "In fact, I've been meaning to tell you how much I admire your designs. They're really very brilliant."

"And I know who you are too. I had the great pleasure to attend one of your concerts with the Toronto Symphony Orchestra and was enthralled by your wonderful talent."

How could he possibly remember my guest appearance with the Toronto Symphony, when I was sixteen, more than ten years ago, two years before I gave up my musical studies? On the other hand, how could he make something like that up? I had no idea but I did know how to respond, "Do you think so, honestly?" all big eyes and faux grateful.

"And entirely from memory—"

"Well, not *entirely*—"

"And the execution . . . not the slightest exaggerated movement."

At the point where further praise threatened to nauseate, I reached into my beaded reticule for a cigarette, pushed it into my holder, and asked for a light. He presented me with one, then mumbled something, lifted his tie, and indicated a speck of sauce that had fallen on it.

"What?" I said without quite understanding why he was showing me his sauce-stained tie.

"Silly of me to have worn my favorite tie, don't you think?"

I leaned over to study it, making a clicking sound with my tongue to express sympathetic awe at the tragedy.

"Maybe not," I said, lifting my head. "Now you have a memento of the evening. Besides, it's a very small spot. Would you like me to have a go at it?"

I still don't know why I said this. Despite having drunk two cocktails, I was not, as I recall, intoxicated. What business did I have offering to help a man whom I had not known longer than a few moments . . . and in such an intimate manner? One thing seemed fairly clear to me, though: my husband-to-be, despite the fact that he was totally lacking in intuition, understood my desire to be of service. Beware of men who would have you inspect food stains on their clothing. It's a test. His hands flew up to the snowy white handkerchief in his jacket pocket. "That would be so kind," he said with a heartbreaking smile. "You are my last hope."

I dipped his handkerchief in water and rubbed, looking straight into his eyes, which were gray-brown and large, while he leaned back in his chair, smiling.

"You know," I said, my voice low, confidential, "you really do have a lovely face."

"Great Scott," he said. "Have I? I'm going right home to have a look at it. I never thought it was worth looking at before."

"I'm not joking," I said. "You really have almost the kindest face I ever saw."

The man beamed. Certainly I had scored a triumph. The following day he called my boss to thank him for inviting me to his party, for making it possible for us to meet, and mentioned what a lovely time he had with me. Then I received a postcard upon which he'd written, "It is always such a pleasure to spend an evening with a beautiful woman," and he invited me to tea at the Empress the next day, and then he invited me to dinner the following week, during which he reached beneath the table and squeezed my hand, and then confessed that he was married, though separated and seeking a divorce from a woman he described as demonic.

Then, five weeks later, after four more evenings with Rats, one of my closest friends, Patricia McClure, telephoned to tell me that there was something I had to know.

"Yes," I said.

"People, I'm afraid, are talking."

"Oh, indeed. About what?"

"You and Francis Rattenbury."

"That," I said as nicely as I could, "is my business."

"No doubt," said Patricia, "but it is also Florrie's; she *is* his wife, you know."

You may be wondering why I was throwing myself at a married man who was almost twice my age. *Why was I throwing myself at him?* All I can say is that I had been married twice before and eligible men seemed in short supply. At the time Rats came into my life I had been conducting a series of almost wretchedly comic affairs, the last with a man in the office where I worked, a charming Irishman who refused to leave his wife, and who had slept—so I reckoned—with half a dozen other women in Kings Row & Co. Can you imagine a woman desperate enough to believe that an Irish Catholic man would leave his wife for her? Well, I was. It was that experience which led me not to mind that Rats was twenty-four years older than I, or that he was almost totally lacking in charm. Now do you understand? I didn't want a young charming man, a man who thought he could have whomever he wanted. I wanted, then, to have a husband who would be faithful, a solid companion, a man who would bring me flowers, remember my birthday, and give me little compliments that would make me feel special. Anyone could see he was in love with me. Wasn't that the most important thing to look for in a husband? Well, surely it was, I'd tell myself. Of course it was. And though I knew this made me appear old-fashioned, I have to admit that I liked that he was so much more accomplished than I—the feeling he provided me of being taken care of. I felt the world was his, the physical word, because he was rich and could buy whatever he wanted, and because trees and rocks and shrubs, his architectural materials, seemed as though they had been expressly created for his use. When the tension of our silences became unbearable, I'd think about the British Columbia Parliament that he had designed, about its cost and historical importance, its many rooms and gardens, and then I'd think I was a lucky woman and was grateful to have him.

Other times, observing other couples in the park, observing how they managed to find so much to talk about, I was not grateful at all.

Rats' divorce was finalized in January 1925, and I was again named "other woman" in the suit, and although I became Mrs. Francis Rattenbury the following year, that did nothing to improve my reputation. My detractors scored a signal victory by denying me membership in the Victoria Musical Society, and when I called Patricia McClure soon after my marriage in an effort to revive our friendship, I would have been wise to have identified myself by some other name:

"Who's calling?" Patricia asked.

"Mrs. Rattenbury," I said, joking.

"Which Mrs. Rattenbury?"

"Why, it's me, my dear, Alma."

"I know only one Mrs. Rattenbury," said Patricia, "and that's

Mrs. Rattenbury of Prospect Place," and she hung up on me.

I felt cheated. And taken aback, and angry, and hurt. After Rats and I married, I assumed that the circumstances of our courtship would be forgiven and forgotten. I'd married a man who could, I thought, overcome any scandal. I should have known better. Whether I married him or not, we stood condemned. In the narrow-minded world of Victoria society, there was something soiled and deficient about us, something that could not be corrected by marriage or money, and everybody knew it, and I knew it. Even the overwhelming beauty and joy of Felix's birth did nothing to improve our social standing.

I see now that it was especially bad for Rats. A year after we married, the man who had been called Canada's preeminent architect could not find a new client if his life depended on it. "They're pretending I'm dead; no one wants anything to do with me anymore!" he exclaimed on more than one occasion. You could mention several factors, factors such as a change in architectural taste—some critics were calling his work prewar, old guard. He had been expecting to be asked to design a government ministry in Vancouver, but a modernist architect somehow came to the front and was given the job instead. Rats became irritable, began making declarations about the deterioration of architectural standards and taste, and his peers began laughing at him. At a dinner in honor of the governor, he decided to get even by loudly and firmly declaring that a façade was more important to a public building than a foundation, and very much so. They laughed at him so mercilessly that he couldn't sleep that night. There was also the embarrassing disclosure that Rats paid an inadequate reward to another architect for a design that he had been commissioned to create but which the second architect claimed was principally his. God knows what wound that inflicted on his reputation, but I believe that the critical thing, what was most central to his professional decline, was his marriage to me. This was Canada, after all, the provinces, where everybody knows your personal affairs and has little else to talk about. Whose lovely forests and vistas reveal nothing of the backbiting that goes on behind closed doors. Whose two rules are that you cover your rear and keep up your front.

So Rats decided to return to England and focus his efforts on my career instead of his. At first, it seemed like a splendid opportunity. Although my first marriage had ended my musical studies—one could go so far as to say I married in order to escape the piano, the hour-by-hour discipline—I continued writing masses of songs, jotting down melodies on menus or the backs of envelopes, whenever they occurred to me, and then adding lyrics at the piano about lost love. Rats said he believed he could recognize without any possible doubt, in my songs, the kind of unabashed romanticism that the public would pay almost anything to hear. He did not believe this in a half-hearted way. He talked about nothing else. And as he talked about it, and as his plans for me slowly began to take shape, I came to see, to my utter astonishment, he had an ambition locked somewhere within him to become an impresario, a kind of British P. T. Barnum with me as his song-writing Jenny Lind. There was a certain pleasure to being a celebrity that had seduced him once and for all, and he was not yet ready to give it up. Without a career of his own to occupy him, launching mine became a constant preoccupation, a lifeline.

We purchased a house on the south coast of England, in Bournemouth. "Villa Madeira" the new house was called. It was not anywhere near as grand as our home in Canada, and by Victoria standards, the new city was tawdry: more cheap hotels and concrete than pine, landscape, and flowers. Where the typical Canadian city gives the impression of being outclassed by the beauty of its natural setting, Bournemouth gave the impression of a city that had been outclassed by its own past. Once it might have been a lovely resort, a place of considerable charm where exciting things were happening. Not any longer. Commerce had taken over, too many bungalows had been built, too many cafes with mirrored crystal balls, and charm had slowly departed. In fairness, the views of the ocean were spectacular; the new house was nicely laid out and built of lovely yellow limestone. Bournemouth also had the advantage of having a world-famous symphony orchestra and was only a couple of hours from London by train. And in the beginning, this quest of Rats' went remarkably and unexpectedly well. Chums of his from Oxford helped him obtain interviews with music publishers, and he did manage to have several of my songs published under the name Lozanne (Rats thought my real name too pedestrian). Many of my songs were recorded, and many more were played live on the BBC, and for a while, there was a new kind of frenzied excitement in our lives. There were invitations, and concerts, and a little more money, and many more parties, and critics called my music "winsome" and "refreshingly unpretentious," and it seemed for a while that the shift in focus from Rats' career to mine could make up for some of the embarrassment he endured.

Of course, it didn't. How could it have, given the unreality of his expectations? When it started to become apparent that my songs were not about to astonish the world, he gradually became more and more convinced that music publishers were making fun of him; he told me that he noticed music publishers' secretaries would snort or sneeze whenever he entered their offices, and he became more and more suspicious and withdrawn. And when, after two years in England, it became clear that the music industry would show only modest interest in my music, he called them idiots and lost all interest.

It is difficult to say what my feelings were. I did adore the recognition at first. I was reminded of the praise and attention I enjoyed as a child for my concert performing. But I also knew that my songs were not clever and high class—at least, not exceptionally clever and high class. So when I realized they weren't going to be as popular as Rats predicted, I wasn't devastated. I was even a little relieved since I hadn't really composed them for the public; I'd composed them for myself.

For a time, Rats considered returning to architecture. He began talking about re-launching his own career in England, sometime in the future, and would spend increasing portions of the day sequestered in his study, attempting to work out new design ideas, dressed as he used to dress to go to his office, in a three-piece gray or blue suit. But he wasn't convincing, not even to himself. He began speaking of himself as an exile once again, as a persecuted man, and in the middle of the night, when the full strength of his despair set in, he would confess that he felt he was only going through the motions, that he was impersonating himself, that he was a spirit, a ghost or shadow of his former self.

It wasn't his body he'd lost, it was a career, but it shook him more than I believed possible. Each sporadic burst of creative energy, each new design he managed to complete, each moment of pride and hope, seemed merely to provide a stopping point on his steady descent. By the end of our third year in England, he looked beaten. So much had changed since we had landed in England, when he was preoccupied with my career, the offers bobbing before him like apples for the picking. He still told me I had the loveliest eyes he had ever seen, that I was the most brilliant woman he had ever known. But he was no longer the sentimental hero of the party; now he moved like a sleepwalker, dragging his melancholy after him like some colossal and demanding pet, conveying exhaustion even as he stirred his tea.

Instead of going to parties or the theater, he would remain in his study until the wee hours drinking tumbler after tumbler of whiskey, his head weaving over his sketchpad. A full night's sleep had become, for him, a distant memory.

Then, four years after we came to England, I told Rats that I wished to redecorate the guest room and then move into it. I wanted a room of my own.

"Why?" he whispered.

"Well, we've both been growing . . . fussier. You know, harder to live with in close quarters." I didn't think of this at the moment as an insensitive thing to say. I thought of it simply as the truth.

Outwardly, he took the news well. The only immediate sign of his discomfiture was his abandonment of our bedroom. That afternoon, with the help of Irene, our housekeeper, he moved all his belongings into his study. And then later that evening he made a single mute protest: "Someday you'll discover," he said, speaking of himself in the third person, which in him was a sign of strong feeling, "you'll discover that your husband dearly loves you, and that your place, your real place, is with him."

Nothing more was said. He refused to express resentment; he glowed with forbearance.

For a fortnight or more, I was delighted that he seemed to accept the change in sleeping arrangements and wanted to go as before. During the third week I started to find his forbearance and chivalry a little disconcerting. By the fourth, suffocation had begun to set in.

Knowing I had hurt him, knowing how difficult it was for him to sleep without me, and then to still receive his compliments, to witness his gestures of attachment—not only did this make me feel like a monster, it made me act like one. I knew I had no right to feel monstrous, but this is how I did feel. His sadness and compliments and refusal to be annoyed had cast me as the unfeeling wife in my eyes, as well, I imagined, in everyone else's. That's what angered me most. I knew that my anger was nothing more than a pathetic reaction to my guilt. Yet everything about him had begun to bother me. His odor, his cough, just the tone of his voice, saying, "Would you see what's bothering Felix," made me cringe.

What did I intend to do about it?

Find some way to survive, some way to distance myself from him without losing my marriage. Having a room of my own, for instance. I imagined that a room of my own might provide the distance I craved. But I was wrong. My craving for distance intensified. Then Felix was hospitalized in Dorchester, and I was forced to fight with Rats in the morning and then sit in silence with him in the car for half the day. It was too much. I couldn't go on like this.

Eight days after the accident I consulted Irene—Irene the loyal, the practical and wise. She would know what to do. I found her sitting at the kitchen table, cutting carrots into little flowers. When I finished describing Rats' opposition to driving me, cataloguing all my complaints about him, she jolted me with some unexpected advice:

"Why don't you hire a chauffeur? A lot of people have one."

I sat still for a moment looking down at the kitchen table, and at the carrots she was cutting. Then I lifted my eyes to stare at her round face, at her round sad cheeks.

"It never occurred to me," I said.

It sounded extravagant. What did we need a chauffeur for? Rats could drive; he may not have enjoyed driving, but he had never had a major accident, and he could drive when he had to, and he had time to spare. It would be an added expense; money was not as plentiful as it once was.

It didn't matter. I liked the idea. I was sick of fighting with him every morning and sick to death of spending half of the rest of the day sitting next to him in the car. But I did not mention this to him; instead I told him how much easier it would be for us to make the trip to the hospital, to visit Felix, all the hospital appointments I needed to make but couldn't if we didn't have a chauffeur. And he seemed to be listening, though as usual when speaking with Rats during this period my voice was going higher and higher, so that at any point I threatened to break off and begin screaming.

"All right, all right," he said, "if you feel that strongly about it," and on April 28, 1934, he placed the following advertisement in the *Bournemouth Daily Echo:* "Daily willing lad, 16-20, for driving. Scout-trained preferred."

Which is how Percy came into my life.

2

He was the first applicant we interviewed; he had a driver's license; his smile, which reflected a desire to please, was reassuring. He smiled well, with good nature. So I told Rats he'd do. It was that simple. The decision had nothing to do with the longing of a middle-aged woman for a handsome young companion.

I soon learned, however, that when two people are alone in a car for extended periods on a daily basis, it is almost impossible to remain impersonal. Particularly when the driver drives as abysmally as Percy—almost always with careening turns, jerky stops, abrupt accelerations. So oblivious was he to speed limits that I could not help laughing (out of fear)—one chilly overcast spring morning—as the car flew over a hill, literally airborne for a split second. But he laughed with me, which made it fun.

No doubt about it, Percy quite cheered me up. After about a month, we got into the habit of joking every day—about his driving, about people we saw on the streets, and about Rats, whom Percy found endlessly amusing. Quite often, when Rats was around, he would have to put his hand over his mouth, as though he were yawning, to cover the smile that stole across his face, as when Rats snapped open his silver cigarette case and offered first, a cigarette, second, a light, and then, the speech on where and how this particular brand of tobacco was grown, why it was superior to anything available in stores, and how it was that this most rare and stellar of tobaccos became available to

Rats—*personally*. Percy referred to Rats as Mr. Hee Haw because of his obviousness, his obduracy and donkey-like laugh. Percy did a fine job too, or at least a cruel one, on Rats' laugh, which was really more like a tic than a laugh, coming out in large wheezes and bursts and sounding rather like a bray.

Percy doing Rats: "Alma, did you know that you have four distinctive smiles, my darling? You have one for joy, pure and simple. (He brays.) Another when you are sad, my darling, and tears come to your eyes. (More braying.) A third when you crave something, when you're being quite greedy. It's when you must have that second helping of cake and nothing will stop you. And then there's that way your lips curl when you're being wicked, when you're poking fun at some old fool like me. (He brays and thrashes his head back and forth.)"

"You don't have a very high opinion of Rats, do you?" I said, laughing, feeling guilty for laughing.

"No, not a high one—quite a low one."

I told Percy that he should give Rats a chance, and asked if he knew how terribly Rats was teased as a child.

No, he said, he didn't.

"The boys at his school used to play ventriloquist and dummy, and would make Rats play the dummy. They called him Mush Mouth because of his cleft palate."

"That might explain his sadistic streak."

"Rats doesn't have a cruel bone in his body," I said, feeling I needed to come to his defense.

"Well, then, it's obvious you've never seen him pinch Irene's buttocks. He pinches her until tears come to her eyes."

"He does not. She would've told me."

"I've seen him take a hot spoon from his tea and hold it against her leg."

I smiled and shook my head, disbelieving, and asked Percy

whether he resented Rats, if perhaps he had an authority issue with him.

"No, I don't think so," he said, "but I do think he's jealous."

"Of you?"

"Yes, of the time I spend with you."

"I doubt it."

"You don't think so?"

"He told me that he thinks you like boys. He says he's sure you're a sissy."

"What do you think?"

"I don't know what to think. Do you?"

"What?"

"Like boys?"

He puffed out his right cheek and then inserted his forefinger into it, making a flatulent sound.

"Pardon?"

"I don't know what to think either," he said without even the hint of a smile.

I couldn't explain to anyone what it was about Percy's conversation that made me look forward to spending time with him. I hesitate to try to explain now. You could not speak to him about serious things, in a straight sober sort of way. He wouldn't allow it, despite the fact that his life had been far from easy. His mother committed suicide. She put a shotgun into her mouth and used her toe to pull the trigger. He tried to make a joke of it by adding that she needed three attempts before hitting her mark. Ordinary troubles were not what he enjoyed telling; he could abide problems only if they had twists—if they were extravagant, ironical. He regarded irony as a kind of moral duty, but the biggest irony of all is that when you got to know him what you found was not a frivolous person at all but one who was deathly serious. He could become tearful in an instant.

I once asked him how he dealt with the grief from his

mother's death. With his eyes at their bluest and roundest, he said that he still talked to her. Every night before he went to bed she visited with him about his day. "Yes, it's me again," she'd say, "I do hope I'm not coming at a bad time. I just wanted to find out if you got the chauffeur position and to see how you're doing."

I asked him to tell me more.

"If you like," he said, "but you have to promise not to take offense, and most of all not to imagine that I think of you in a morbid way."

"All right," I said, "I promise."

"You resemble her, the same smile."

That was how he talked to me. He had a way of describing things as though I were on his mind, not so much how something was—his mother, a landscape, an event—but how it might connect to me. "She's like you . . . you'd love it . . . it would have charmed you," he said.

One evening, driving in silence through the blackness of a fir-shaded road, where ancient gravestones gloomed through openings in the forest, he said he wished the car had a radio. When the car came out again into the comparative brightness of fields, he added, "I once heard one of your songs on the radio."

"You didn't?" I said, almost astonished that he knew this part of me.

"Yes, I did," he said, looking at me through the rearview mirror. "A song about someone named Marie."

"What did you think of it?" I said.

"I liked it."

"Oh?"

"Yes, I liked it a great deal. How does it go?"

"You're not asking me to recite it, are you?"

"No, I am asking you to sing it. Would you?"

He continued to look at me through the rearview mirror and

I shut my eyes against the persecution of his gaze, and sank a little lower in my seat as though to tell him, and remind myself, that I'm a small and inconsequential person, not to be seen, too inconsequential to be heard, until finally I sighed, "Oh, all right if you insist, but just this one time."

I know it sounds odd to sing for one's chauffeur. However, it embarrasses me now to recall the episode, not so much because I gave in to his request, but because I acted as though he were torturing me, when in truth I can't remember when I'd been more flattered. I sang softly:

> *Are you waiting in your garden*
> *By the deep wide azure sea?*
> *Are you waiting for your loveship*
> *Dark-haired Marie?*

> *I shall come to claim you someday,*
> *In my arms you'll be,*
> *I shall kiss your lips and love you,*
> *Dark-haired Marie.*

I opened the car window. It was eight o'clock, the sun a pink seashell. Beyond the jagged outline of farmhouses the lights from the town flickered whitely, dimly; the smell of lilacs drifted into the car in an invisible mist. Looking back, I'm amazed at the pleasure with which I sang, my lack of self-consciousness. I wasn't worried about appearing absurd. A middle-aged woman attempting to seduce her seventeen-year-old chauffeur. That notion didn't enter my head. I experienced only the music flowing through me and his wish to hear me sing.

I wasn't in love with him. But I did love the way he made me feel: the camaraderie of our automobile trips, the feelings of ease and lightness he gave me. Most of all, I loved his special power of deflection: his ability to shift my focus away from Felix and Rats and onto things that were simpler and less painful. I stopped worrying about Felix's rate of recuperation which was slower than expected. I'd sit calmly through dinner with Rats and not get annoyed by his endearments or his chewing sounds. Nothing he did bothered me any longer. It was as though all my tension and restlessness had resolved themselves into a single focus: this boy, our drives, the places to which we had been and where we would go. Everything else seemed insignificant.

3

This was the state in which things stood one far-too-humid afternoon in mid-July. It was five o'clock, the heat suspended in the air like sediment in a pond. "Stroke weather" my mother used to call it; "gnat weather" too. We were returning from an expedition to London, where we had gone to drop off Irene for a visit to her cousin's, and were about thirty miles outside of Bath, on a road that was mostly unpaved, when the engine died.

"Why are we stopping?" I said.

Percy sat still a moment. Nothing seemed amiss except a faint smell of burning rubber; that was all. Then he said, "I'm going to have a look," and got out of the car and raised the hood. I wouldn't have thought he even knew how to raise the hood. His head and shoulders disappeared beneath it, as did his hands and arms. Minutes passed with him staring at the engine in silence. I called to him: "What on earth are you looking at?" He seemed not to hear me. Then he closed the hood, got back inside, and turned on the ignition.

It started up again.

We drove, relatively smoothly, for about a hundred yards, but then lost speed, lost heart, and jerked to a stop again. Percy was able to restart it, with the identical result. Then, after about a half dozen restarts and stops, the burning rubber smell growing progressively more intense, he gave up.

I might have even been amused by the situation had I been

comfortable enough to feel amusement, but I was not at all comfortable. I could feel perspiration already wetting my brows and trickling into my eyes, my bottom both itched and ached, and I was afraid that the black dye on my eyelashes would dissolve at any moment. I took the powder compact from my purse, opened it, and squinted into the small round mirror. I could recognize the growing pouches under my eyes, those parts of me that I had been spending so much time of late camouflaging and deploring. My hair was still there, looking dull and practically uncombed. And my eyeliner, it was there too, intact. Thank God for small consolations.

I got out of the car, took off my round-brimmed straw hat and fanned myself as I looked around. England had never seemed so unattractive: up ahead I saw a stand of dark cedar, a patch of swamp, and fields covered with bare stalks and various tattered plants; in the other direction, the road descended into pasture, more pasture, huddles of ragged goats and ponies, and what appeared to be a narrow farmer's cottage with walls of wattle and daub.

A hot breeze stirred the insect population.

"Alma, this is the most dismal part of England I've ever seen." He was sitting on the running board, his long legs stretched out as if disgust had reached his very toes. "What a place to end up."

On the other side of the road, several crows were pecking at a furry mound of hedgehog.

"Crows too," he said waving in their direction.

"We haven't ended up anywhere yet," I said. "We can easily walk down the hill to the cottage and ask for help."

"All right," he said, "but I think only I should go since you're wearing high heels."

I was wearing the wrong shoes. The only sensible course of action would have been to wait for Percy to return. But I did not like the idea of waiting. "I think I can manage on them," I said.

"You'll break your ankle."

"You are sweet," I said, not relishing the walk, but not wanting to stay put either. "You *are* a dear," I said, putting my arms around his neck and kissing him firmly on the cheek, "but I don't intend to sit here quietly and bake while you go off and get lost." There was no shade on either side of the road, and the gnats were so plentiful it was hard to keep them out of my eyes. "We're going together."

Percy walked and I staggered through a patch of road pocked with fist-sized holes—a distance of about twenty yards. Then he stopped. "This isn't going to work. Face it: you can't walk. You simply cannot."

"Waiting makes me feel helpless and useless. I refuse."

"If a car comes by, you can flag it down. That would be a major contribution. You can make believe you're Dark-haired Marie. Waiting for her loveship by the deep wide azure sea."

"Are you making fun of my song?"

He shook his head, smiled.

"I thought you *loved* my song."

"Alma, you're so odd."

"Shall I sing it for you? Would that satisfy you?"

It was not believable. The sun was burning, gnats were biting, my shoes were coming off, and my ankles hurting. I was dazed, sweating, melting in the heat but at some point in this oppressive situation, I had begun to enjoy the challenge of being *that* oppressed. I felt like a character in a black comedy. We were on a remote highway, no other people around. It was just the two of us. Nevertheless, I imagined we were on stage and the road we were walking on was not a road but a theater, and the sun was not the sun but a spotlight rendering us absurdly, outrageously visible.

I took off my shoes. I ran back to the Daimler with short quick steps, my skirt hitched up round my knees like a pair of knickers, and tossed the shoes inside, determined to walk to the cottage barefoot, when I saw a sight that made me pause.

A car in the distance. But not just a car—it was a car that was moving along the road at high speed, coming toward us from the London direction, growing larger and more distinct by the moment, till at a distance of about two city blocks I could make out the shape of the grille. No, it couldn't be!

Percy stepped into the middle of the road in front of me and held up his hand. Yes, it was! A Bentley! A cream-and-chocolate Bentley!

The car slowed, pebbles crunching beneath its tires. The driver was an elderly Scot with a stubble of white beard and a Pomeranian beside him on the front seat.

He said he would be more than happy to give us a ride into Bath, if that would help.

"Gorgeous car," Percy called out as he ran back to the Daimler to retrieve my shoes, and the two of us got into the rear seat of the Bentley, which was upholstered in dark-brown leather. The whole interior more resembled my notion of a luxury yacht than of a car. How wonderful to be back in the world of beautiful things! I rolled my window down the better to see the barns and thick-chested ponies that lined the road. I rode like that watching the ponies and barns march backward, a glittering confidence taking hold of me, which may account for why I introduced Percy to the Scot as my brother. I knew that I shouldn't have but I wanted to. It was all done in a moment. And what a liberating, inspired moment it seemed! Percy, who pressed my arm as he lounged back in the car, wasn't wearing a chauffeur's uniform, just an ordinary gray suit and didn't look like a chauffeur. I told myself there was nothing to be gained by telling the truth except embarrassment for Percy, especially since the Scot appeared more than content to entertain us, nonstop, with his views on psychoanalysis, treating us to the dullest and most embarrassing of confidences about his experiences as an analysand.

He let us out in Bath, at the Queens Hotel. We entered the huge Victorian foyer with its ferns and grandfather clocks and mahogany woodwork, at six-forty, and I used the phone at the desk to call Rats to explain that the car had broken down. I told him I was safe, but that Percy and I would have to remain in Bath until we could get the car repaired. He approved. What else could he do?

Then, as Percy and I exchanged smiles, we checked in as brother and sister. In my mind, it had the attraction of a conspiracy, a game that was amusing because subversive. But subversive how? Subversive of what? I didn't in the least care. It had been one of the marvels of our relationship that from the first, Percy, so much younger, more playful, more whimsical than I, instead of aging me by the contrast, infused me with a desire to match his own gaiety and playfulness.

Which doesn't, of course, suffice as an explanation. What could? It was an absurd thing to do. In my defense, it did occur to me how incredibly embarrassing it would be if we ran into the Scot in Bath and he were to discover that Percy was in fact my chauffeur.

At the same time, my almost total imperviousness to embarrassment amazed me. Ever since my divorce from my second husband I'd been tormented by a sort of apprehensive dread that I'd be exposed in some way, found undeserving or lacking. It began even before my divorce. It began with my concert career. Ever since I began playing the piano in recitals, I couldn't remember a moment when I hadn't worried about hitting the wrong note. Before concerts I used to pray to God to guide my hands and keep me from humiliating myself—and then, gradually, it wasn't only my musicianship which would trouble me, but something I might say, or something about my makeup or clothing.

But not that evening. I felt this sense of triumph—the same feeling I had when I ran away to marry my first husband—as though I had at last thrown down the gauntlet to my fears, my forced respectability, the imperatives to be prudent and appear perfect.

There is a freedom in being stranded: When no one knows you, you can do what you like.

In the hotel lift, a wizened old woman with ear lobes that hung like stones and her nearly identical female companion gave us appraising looks. Two wrinkled old women with unhealthy-looking yellowish skin. Perhaps they had mistaken me for a prostitute with her customer since we had no luggage. The bellhop was taking us to our room empty-handed. Perhaps the old women didn't care at all for the way I was dressed—too brightly, in blue silk covered with blue-and-gold gardenias. Or perhaps the old ladies were shocked because I was having difficulty stifling my laughter. Nothing was funny. Then what was I laughing at? What were both of us laughing at? I couldn't believe how inappropriately I was acting, how childishly. I was a wife and mother, the mistress of the Villa Madeira, a woman of substance, but that moment I didn't feel like a woman of substance. I felt lighter than air, as if I'd suddenly become porous, as if the solids in me had been replaced by hydrogen.

How astonishingly strange to be sharing a hotel room with Percy! But there we were, in a lovely room with high ceilings, lovely floral wallpaper, and curtains of green-and-mulberry brocade. Outside, the wrought-iron balcony and shimmering moonlight. Below, Bath twinkling in the evening heat, its street-lamps giving off a soft-edged glow that made the city seem part of another era, like a painting in a museum, an expression of myth.

Percy stalked around the room in his bare feet, opening the dressing table, the bureau, the closet, touching the tulip-shaped reading lamps, the little powder jars in the bathroom, the scent bottles and little china ring tree, running his fingers along every plane as though he were exploring the interior of an enchanted palace built expressly for us. "What a bed!" he said, setting his teeth and bouncing on the edge of one of the room's two beds. "This is going to be sensational!"

Of course, we would sleep in separate beds, though this had not been said. Remember, I didn't imagine myself attracted to him in *that* way. But after I'd washed myself, arranged my face and tied my hair, pulling it back and pinning it up, and Percy put his shoes and jacket back on, in preparation for supper at the Starlight Pavillion, there was a moment when I pretended that this was indeed our enchanted palace, had always been, and whatever we wanted to do here, we could. I slipped my arm through his. I turned my head to watch him. Close up, he seemed so familiar, the unlined forehead and cheeks the texture of rich cream, not my pretend brother but my real one. His skin seemed beautiful to me. Really, I thought, most women would find him exceptionally handsome.

He hesitated at the door, patted down his hair. I wanted to pat his hair too, just give it a pat. Then we walked into the lift and through the brilliantly lit lobby and into the dining room, arms linked, all at once enfolded in candlelight, white linen, green bottles in buckets of ice, the tinkle and chime of glass and china.

There were a great many diners in the room conversing in low tones, most of them, perhaps all, more beautifully and formally attired than us. Some stared. What was there to see? A middle-aged woman, her sleeveless dress slightly wilted, the bodice hanging droopily over her breasts, sharing champagne and veal with her younger brother. Nothing terribly bizarre there, nothing could be more forgettable.

We sat by a window overlooking a stone balustrade, near the small chamber ensemble. The music made me reminisce about my song-writing efforts, and I told Percy that I thought I might be able to compose again. When I recognized the undulating repetitions of Borodin's string quartet, I became certain of it. I shut my eyes, the better to concentrate, and became so lost in the music, that I did indeed more or less totally forget Percy.

But then I opened my eyes, and he was there. His pale, light, clear blue-gray eyes watching me. He had been sitting there doing nothing, just sitting there in his chair, staring at my face.

"I thought you were asleep," he said.

Why did I find it so flattering, the idea that he would gaze at me in my sleep? Did I imagine he found me alluring? Or that he saw in me a special friend? Had his gaze any message for me? I did not know. But I had no misgivings: I allowed myself to be enchanted.

I smiled at him, and lifted my glass. He clinked my glass with his, and returned my smile. And then I did something completely uncharacteristic: I put my hand on his knee and squeezed. His eyes skipped down to look at my hand and then went back up to my eyes. A faint tremble at the corners of his smile seemed to say that he was aware of the gesture, that he took it in, and that it was significant to him.

Then the waiter stepped out of nowhere, soft and deft as a cat. "Pardon me, madam, but—ah—is there anything else you'll be needing?"

I pulled my hand back quickly—too quickly—and for a moment couldn't think to answer. "No," I said at last, and told him to put the bill on my room.

The thought that the waiters and other diners might think

me inappropriate hit me with the force of something coming from outside. Really, I had no business squeezing his knee. It was an absurdly lascivious gesture. Even if people believed that we were siblings, was that any way for an older sister to behave? And I had a frightful, sickening vision of the other waiters telling each other, amidst roars of laughter, precisely what I'd been doing with Percy's knee. She *couldn't*—she *couldn't* have done that!

Not wanting to contemplate my sudden lapse from grace, I suggested we call it a night.

He rose, silently. I wondered whether conversation was called for, after squeezing his knee, in such a place, and rose silently, too. And as we walked in silence, our heads bowed, our arms clinging to our sides, I who had been so light a little while ago, felt unaccountably tired. And the longer the silence between us continued, the more aware I became of what I must look like to others: the impossibility of my dress, our age difference, and the absurdity of sharing a bottle of champagne and clinking glasses with my chauffeur. To me, a shaft of light circled us as we walked through the hotel corridors, past reception rooms, reading rooms, billiards rooms. I felt again as though I was on stage, but now everyone was staring at us with amused, appraising eyes. Surely, everyone we passed knew about Percy and me, and that there was something amiss in our relationship.

And I saw most clearly for the first time how humiliating the actual experience of sharing a room with him might be. Perhaps he would see me in an unpleasantly revealing way—undressed perhaps, or partially undressed, since I did not bring any nightwear. Perhaps he would see the loose flesh on my abdomen, or on my thighs and hips. Or my mouth would remain open in sleep. Or I'd snore.

When we got back to our room, Percy bolted the door behind him and asked what we should do now.

"I'm taking a bath," I said crisply, and escaped into the bathroom where I drew a bath for myself and soaked for a long time. After washing out my under things, wringing them out and hanging them up to dry, and wrapping a towel around myself, I got into one of the beds, the one Percy was not inhabiting, and turned my face away from him and closed my eyes.

I bade him goodnight and said I'd see him in the morning.

"Goodnight," he whispered back. He had been lying down on top of his bed doing nothing, just lying there, staring at the wall.

And as I lay there, trying to sleep, I could not help listening to him get up to use the bathroom, the creaking of floorboards, the sound of water rushing through pipes; then him returning to bed and tossing: sheets rustling, the bed squeaking, and him sighing. At last, after what seemed like hours, he quieted down, not a sound coming from him but gentle, subdued, rhythmic breathing. He seemed to have fallen asleep.

What was I doing when he seemed to sleep? Not sleeping. Worrying. Worrying about sleeping in the same room as he, and wishing I were not.

Then, I again heard the rustle of sheets, the squeak of his bed. Then steps and his voice:

"Alma?"

I made no move, no sound.

"Oh, Alma—are you awake?"

He had walked across the room. He was wearing only his shirt, and seemed to me thinner, ganglier, more awkward in shape and motion, than I had ever seen him. I had a skeleton before me. With the indirect light from the window turning his pale flesh sallow, he looked positively alarming.

I clenched my hands on the sheet, and considered my options. I could point silently but dramatically to his bed. I could shut my eyes and pretend I was still asleep. Or I could keep my eyes open and wait to see what he intended to do. But what if he didn't do anything? What if he just stayed where he was, hovering by my bed? Best to tell him right now to cut it out and get back into his own bed.

This I did, firmly, adding, "Now if you don't mind, I'd like to get some sleep."

"Why," came his soft voice. "Why, what have I done?"

The thought that he'd feel responsible for the general downturn of my mood hadn't occurred to me, but it occurred to me then, and suddenly it seemed horribly unfair to have snapped at him, and also to have kept my distance from him after dinner. God, I'm a bitch, I thought, a horrible, unfeeling bitch.

"Why," he said again. "Why are you so angry at me?"

I sat up, my hands lying open on my lap. "Why on earth would I be angry? You've been great, I mean that."

He drew a step nearer. "You say, 'You've been great,' but the way you just said, 'Now if you don't mind, I'd like to get some sleep,' made it sound as though you're really irritated with me."

"Foo," I said, laughing.

"You resent being stuck here with me."

"Will you stop it?"

"One minute you seem furious at me and the next you're telling me you think I've been great. I'm completely confused."

"Sorry about that. I hope it's not fatal."

"Why do you want me here with you? I'd really like to know."

"Because I do," I laughed again.

He was standing quite close now, touching my pillowcase with the tips of his fingers in an attitude of such unabashed desolation that I felt something collapse inside me, and without thinking about what I was letting myself in for, I took his ice-cold hand into both of mine and said, "Why don't you just lie down beside me and try to get some sleep."

He hesitated.

"It's all right," I said, and shut my eyes, and repeated in a voice that was half solace, half command, "It'll be all right."

"Are you sure?" he asked.

I shifted to give him room, "Of course, I'm sure. Now come." And he got in beside me, nestled against me, in the crook between my breast and shoulder, and let me kiss his temples and cheeks, and I thought, Oh, Christ, I'm making love with a chauffeur—*my seventeen-year-old chauffeur!*

He nestled against me, burrowing into me like a rooting animal. Seventeen years old, I thought, and wondered whether he was with me now as a man or boy. Then he found my nipple and I had the answer, and my heart reeled with the sweetness of it.

When I awoke the next morning, I lay still with my eyes closed trying to remember the night before. Could I have imagined it? I reached out a hand across the bed. Where was he? Then I heard the sound of splashing water.

I opened my eyes and saw him in the bathroom, shirtless, his jutting ribs and starved shoulders making him look like the photographs of people from underprivileged countries.

I spoke quietly, hesitantly. "I was wondering what time it is."

No reply.

I spoke more loudly: "I can't believe what happened last night . . . what we did."

He emerged from the bathroom patting himself dry with a towel.

"I can't either."

"You must think I'm an immoral woman. Have I lost all dignity? Do you despise me now?"

He shook his head no.

"Well, did you enjoy it?" I asked him, heaving myself up a little on the bed, pulling the sheet up to cover my chest, thinking the question ridiculous.

A sad smile appeared on his face; he leaned against the bathroom door. "Enjoy it? How could I not have enjoyed it?"

"I'm very old, you know."

"How silly. You're not old. You're beautiful. *This* is so beautiful, being alone with you here. I can't keep away from you," and he came over and kneeled beside me.

I said, "May I ask you something? You don't have to answer if it embarrasses you."

"Of course."

"Have you ever slept with a woman before?"

"I never touched a woman before."

"My Lord!" I said, and slid my hand softly over his face, my fingertips catching on the side of his mouth. And then I added, with a note of guilt that was surprising, that I had never before heard in my voice when speaking with him—and surprised too, to find that I was speaking, thus guiltily, no more than the obvious, "Maybe I shouldn't have."

"Shouldn't have what?"

"Seduced you."

"I seduced *you*," he said. "And I've never felt so sure about anything in my whole life." Then he put his arms around my waist, pressed his cheek against my chest, and said, "Did you know that I love you more than anyone?"

Did you know that I love you more than anyone?

"No," I said. But I felt no surprise, only a vague sense of dread, a longing not to be told, and beyond this I remember wondering what he meant, whether he meant he loved me more than he loved anyone, or more than anyone loved me. I still don't know which it was, or indeed whether he might have meant both, but I knew it was not the sort of thing I was used to hearing from him. He seemed, in a way, desperate. What had happened to his sense of humor, his irony? Laughter—the thing that brought us together—seemed to have withdrawn into some dark hole.

While we held each other, while I stroked his back with the palms of my hands, I tried to figure out what had happened—and was happening. Though Percy said he loved me, I was afraid that he might come to regret last night. And I was afraid that he might not. Could he handle having a lover who was his employer, and an employer who was his lover? I wanted him to want me—to seriously want me, but I also wanted him to continue wanting me as he had in the past: lightly, playfully.

Still more disquieting, I did not know precisely what I was capable of. Could I embark seriously on a love affair with a man who lived in the same home as my husband? I did have my own bedroom, with Rats situated on a completely separate floor, and it would be easy enough to make excuses to go on daylong excursions with Percy, since he was my chauffeur. But was I capable of leading a double life? Was I capable of doing what Anna Karenina and Madame Bovary had done?

No, I didn't think I was, especially since both those novels ended in the woman committing suicide.

On the other hand, adultery was something I did have some experience with—before my marriage to Rats, that is. When I worked as a secretary, I had slept with several married men, although I could not repress a shiver at the memory, recalling how poorly I handled that period of my life. I had been dishonest, irresponsible, and selfish.

And now, look at me, for all my experience and lack of success, committing adultery again.

Lord, I was lost. Have pity on me! For despite the obvious need for restraint, I couldn't tear myself away. Even as I said to myself, I have shared a hotel room with my chauffeur and made love with him, and my life will now be impossible, I kept right on kneading and squeezing his back, enveloping him, overwhelmed by the feel of him, as if I had never known until that moment the feel of a man's body. My legs gripped him. I knew I had to let him go, put an end to it once and for all, but every time I lifted one of my legs, it returned to him. Every time I tried to sit up, I fell back onto the bed.

And the more I failed, the more I rationalized. I know this is insane, I told myself, but didn't we already do it last night? And aren't we on the bed, already halfway there? So what's the difference? What's the harm in doing it one more time? Just this one time. This one morning. Goddamn it, I want to. I don't care.

And while we were doing it, I didn't care. But afterward, as we were lying side by side, facing the French doors, the bright sunlight hitting us almost in the face, I told him that we were not under any circumstances to sleep with each other again.

Minutes passed. Then:

"Alma," he said plaintively.

"Yes," I said.

"Tell me why we can't sleep together again." His voice sounded weak and like the voice of somebody else.

I said, "I'm old enough to be your mother."

"So what?"

"Did you know it's against the law to have sex with your mother?"

"What's the rest of it?"

"Does there have to be more?" I said, wrapping my arms around his head, clutching him against my chest. "I've made a lot of mistakes in my life. Many would say sleeping with you is the worst. Most would say it. But to me the worst mistake of all is the one I want to make, yet know I shouldn't, and that is to sleep with you again."

"My sweaty Mama," Percy said, running his hand over my moist stomach and kissing my breast. "I don't want to stop."

I closed my eyes and whispered, "Neither do I." My body was melting from the heat, my throat dry. "But we have to," I said, and began to rock him back and forth, back and forth, until my eyes filled with tears.

"I don't think I *can* stop," he said in that weak voice again, and buried his face against my breast.

This is where I went to pieces. I couldn't help feeling guilty and started to plead. And my pleading seemed to go on forever; there was no end to it, no end to the calamities that I listed for us if we were to sleep with each other again: dogs would bark at us, children would follow us up and down the street mocking us, he would be fired, I would end up on the street or in a loony bin nothing but a wizened old hag, and the worst calamity of all, a calamity that seemed so painful and went so deep that I doubted I could survive if it were to occur: I'd lose Felix.

Percy lifted his head and looked at me. There was no color in his face; his face looked thinner. It was as though he had aged in the last few moments and I had an old man before me.

"Yes, Alma . . . yes, I understand . . . you're right. We can't do this again."

4

But we did. What can I say? It's not like I didn't want to stop. It's just that whenever I tried, whatever I told myself, whether I made promises to myself or pacts with God, I always found loopholes. *I'll just lie with Percy and cuddle, that's all I'll do. I've had a really exhausting day; I just need company tonight. It's no more than a trifle: just a warm body in bed so I can have a good night's sleep. It makes sense.*

And it did in a way; I did sleep better with him.

After we got back to the Villa Madeira, I did not ask Percy to come to my bedroom for an entire week, and then I did not ask him to come for three nights. Then it was two nights, then I found myself not asking every other night, and finally, after a month, it did not matter whether I asked or not. He came anyway.

I developed a long list of reasons to not object, a growing list. A bad marriage. An impossible husband. A disappointing career. *So I have a lover; it's only fair. I deserve one. So what if Percy lacks even the minimum credentials to qualify as a mature adult? I can be a child with him. So what if Rats finds out? He probably already knows.*

I said this to myself with increasing conviction. I mean, how likely is it that Rats, whose study is right below my bedroom, would fail to hear footsteps over his head whenever Percy comes into my room? How likely that he wouldn't hear our occasional loud conversations? If you consider that the Villa Madeira is not

45

a large house and that only four adults live in it, you would have to say it is highly unlikely. And yet there was not even a hint of an accusation, not a word said that I might've wished unsaid. Rats' mood, in fact, seemed much improved.

So what's to prevent us—Rats, Percy, and me—from continuing just as we are?

This is what I told myself. This is what I struggled to believe. And then, suddenly, I couldn't do it any longer. My capacity for self-deception collapsed.

It began with an argument in our car.

One afternoon near the beginning of October—this was two weeks after Felix returned from the hospital—Percy was collecting brush in the yard. He was in his shirtsleeves, his sleeves rolled to the elbow, looking very busy, active and intent. I came out to see if he needed help carrying the brush to the back of the garage. I tiptoed up to him from behind and put my arms gently around his waist. When I kissed the back of his neck and his cheek, he turned to me, took me in his arms, and we stood for a long while without moving.

Then, pulling back suddenly, he said:

"Hey, Alma, when was the last time we drove anywhere? Come on. Let's drive to the Cotswolds tomorrow?"

"Tomorrow?"

"Why not? Wouldn't you love to have a picnic out on the fairy hills?"

"We can't tomorrow," I said. "Don't you remember? You have to drive Rats and me to Winchester." I reminded him that we had planned a dinner engagement with the Wyatts, a couple Rats and I had known in Italy.

"Oh come on, you can get out of it. Tell him you have a doctor's appointment or something."

"I can't, Percy. Rats hardly ever agrees to visit people, so this is really quite special for him. He's been talking about it for weeks. You know how he is sometimes. It's like dealing with a child. Besides, we'd be disappointing the Wyatts if we canceled. Rats and I stayed with them in Capri. I told you about it, that time Rats broke his ankle. They practically saved his life."

His eyes, partly hidden by the mass of hair that came down over his forehead as he stooped to pick up an armful of brush, were ostentatiously mournful, as though he was assuming the expression on purpose. He carried the brush behind the garage, where he laid it near an old gas tank. I also picked up a load of brush and carried it behind the garage, clasping it to my chest with both hands.

"I'm sure we can handle a short postponement," I said, after I'd dropped my bundle. "We can go to the Cotswolds in a day or two."

"I guess so."

"So why the long face?"

"Nothing. Really, nothing. I don't want you to get in trouble with the Wyatts or disappoint Rats. I guess I was just thinking how wonderful it would be to spend a day with you, to have you all to myself. That's all."

"Oh, Percy, that's so lovely," I said, "I wish we could go to the Cotswolds tomorrow, but I'm afraid we'll have to put it off for a little while. We have to, darling."

The next day, on the drive out to the Wyatts, there was tension in the air, which I could sense even though there wasn't any actual conflict. Percy's expression, usually so light and engaging, had darkened. He did not smile or look at me. All he did was drive: hunched over slightly, both hands gripping the wheel. He kept to the speed limit, accelerating more smoothly and turning corners more carefully than was his custom. But he was muttering to himself, his lips shaping words he didn't say out loud. He was polite, but also, in an odd way, not there.

Rats, for his part, talked more than usual. He seemed excited by the prospect of visiting his friends, whom he called his "angels of mercy," and even told a few jokes about women. Which, for me, was one of the great mysteries of his personality, how in the midst of heaping upon women the most sublime compliments, he would suddenly start talking about us as if we were a lower life form.

The visit to the Wyatts went unusually well. Rats ate and drank and chattered with unwonted sparkle, as if he were back to his old self again. It wasn't until the return trip—until the time, in fact, when we had to drive through a rainstorm, and it was almost too noisy to talk in the car—that the first faint discordances crept into our conversation. I don't remember exactly how it started. Rats may have asked Percy about a turn he thought he should have taken, and Percy may have answered by saying that the turn was not coming up quite yet but in a few miles. I honestly don't remember. But it prompted Rats to tell Percy that he thought it was a good thing he was an architect and not a chauffeur, which somehow led him to explain to Percy how he began his career as an architect. Besides the fact that I was completely bored by his conversation, it was raining brutally hard, bullets of rain beating down on the roof of the car, so that I hardly heard a word Rats said. But then I thought I heard Rats ask Percy something personal about himself.

"What?" Percy said. "I missed that."

"Chauffeuring," Rats said, leaning toward Percy. "Do you plan on ever doing something with your life other than chauffeuring?"

"Yes, yes," Percy yelled back. "Something a bit more lucrative."

"You're not looking for another position now, are you?"

"What?" Percy said again, although I didn't have any trouble hearing him.

"Another position," Rats yelled. "Are you looking for

something else?"

"No," Percy said, "not for the moment."

"I have to give you credit. I don't know if I could handle it—working as somebody's servant. I'd sooner throw myself out of a window."

"Throw yourself out of a window?" Percy said.

"What did you say?"

"I said—throw yourself out of a window?"

"Yes, throw myself out a window. What I'm asking, Percy, is how you can stand being given orders and treated as an inferior? It would drive me mad. I suppose you must begin to wonder sometimes if you really *are* inferior?"

Percy said no, he never thought of himself as inferior. Being a chauffeur, it's just a job to him.

"Just a job?" Rats seemed offended. "Then why do you do it?"

The sky went white and thunder quickly followed, a distant blasting and cracking.

This, I thought, is an opportunity to redirect the conversation. "Oh, Jesus, *listen*," I cried, sitting up straight in the back seat and peering through a window out of which I could see almost nothing. "The sky is falling down! Maybe we'll have to stay overnight at an inn. Wouldn't that be awful?"

"To earn a living," Percy said to Rats, "why else would someone be a chauffeur?"

"The trouble with you, Percy, you don't have any ambition. You think you can get through life without doing any work."

There was a silence for a few moments. I dared not risk the slightest movement, for fear an inhalation of air, a jab of my elbow, might be enough to rouse my husband to make additional commentary on Percy's character.

No such luck.

"Man does not live by bread alone, Percy. Don't you forget

that. A woman can be satisfied with children and a home, but a man has to have some pride in his occupation."

I said it was nonsense, the idea that women can be satisfied more easily than men.

"Nonsense? I think not."

"It's insulting to women."

"On the contrary, my darling, it is the greatest compliment to women I could pay."

"What do you, as a man, know about women's feelings?"

"I think men have the right to express their views on women just as women have the right to express their views on men, and if, like everyone else, I want to state my opinion, then—"

"No one's saying you don't have a right to your opinion," I said, cutting him off. "You're merely being asked to be more thoughtful, not to ramble on about women's feelings as if you were an expert on them, because whether you see it or not you're acting as if you're quite superior."

"Oh, all right, all right—" Rats bowed his head and lifted his hands as if attempting to ward off an incoming blow. "No need to get all riled up now. I've just been trying to give Percy a little helpful advice, that's all."

"You're awfully irritating when you're determined to be help-ful," I said. "You go too far, darling."

"Has everything I've said been very, very irritating to you, Percy?"

"No . . . I mean, that's all right, sir."

I tried to think of something else to say, and while I was try-ing, Rats readied himself to tell a joke. The symptoms were all there: the slight heaving of the chest, the clearing of the throat, the anticipatory licking of the lips.

"Why did the woman cross the road?"

I bit: in order to get it over with as quickly as possible. "I have no idea," I said. "Why?"

"I have no idea either," said Rats. "What I want to know is what she was doing out of the kitchen?"

That should have ended it. Rats brayed immoderately. His body twitched and rumbled, and then he began to nod his head slowly and steadily, and I thought he was going to drop off to sleep. But it seems he was only thinking, because then he said, "Percy, I don't mean to stick my nose into your affairs, but there's one small point I'm just not getting. What exactly do you plan to do with yourself in the long term? You see, I'm having a bit of difficulty seeing you languishing indefinitely behind the wheel of some automobile while other men your age are advancing themselves by getting an education or whatever—but that's the point, you see. Do you see what I'm leading to?"

"No, sir."

"You have to do something with your life. You have to choose a direction. So what will it be? A secretary? A bookkeeper? What?"

I waited.

Percy didn't answer.

"Everyone wants to know how in the world I was in a position to be asked to design the British Columbia Parliament."

"Everyone?" I asked, trying to sound convivial, though I really wanted to crawl away and hide, though what I really wanted to say was: Could you please stop talking, Rats, before you drive me crazy.

"It's because of my training," he said. "I was trained at the University. Now do you see where I'm heading?"

"I haven't the faintest idea," I answered.

Rats ignored me and spoke only to Percy. "Assuming for the moment there's a true vocation lying in wait for you somewhere, Percy, don't you think you'd be more apt to discover it at a college or university than behind the wheel of somebody's car? As a young man with your whole life in front of you, don't you think, in all sincerity, that you owe it to yourself to give a little thought to returning to school? And I believe you owe it to somebody else, too. I believe—" He lowered his voice. "I believe you owe it to your mum. I'm sure it would make her proud if she were alive to see you return to school and make a future for yourself."

The recipient of this advice stiffened in his seat; his hands gripped the wheel like claws.

At this point we were driving along Cheriton Bridge Road where it leaves the Westminster Forest Road and begins to border the Great Crown Reservoir, dark and turbulent and almost overflowing.

"Rats, darling," I said, in a tinsel bright voice, "you're doing it again. You're insisting on helping a blind man through traffic though he's not blind and doesn't want to cross the street."

"Well," Rats said to Percy, disregarding my comment, "what do you think?"

"I don't think so," said Percy.

"Why not?" Rats said. "I'm telling you, if you took a business class or two, you could get a job as a clerk or a secretary or something like that. You could have a bit of dignity."

"Business school is very expensive, Rats," I said.

"Oh, I know," he said. "I didn't mean now. I meant as a long-term goal. I just think it would be nice for Percy to have something to work for and look forward to. I know he can't afford it now."

Rats was not a man to look for trouble. He was an innocent, a man who didn't know that people have extremely delicate feelings. He simply had no idea. But this was more than ingenuousness, it was something like arrogance: Rats seemed determined to demonstrate his sophistication at Percy's expense. It was as though he was showing off his enormous career credits by comparing himself to someone who had no credits at all, someone who was a boy, a twig. And that reference to Percy's mother—my God! Where did that come from? It was completely out of line. Ah yes, I told myself. Never underestimate the cruelty in a man's heart. Rats had to be stopped, but every time I said something about the Wyatts or the weather or something on an entirely different subject, making a great show of laughing and exclaiming, he interrupted with something about the career and future he assumed Percy should want. He was like an old record turning round and round on the same groove. Meanwhile, Percy just sat there driving, looking straight ahead, but apparently stewing, because he said something that nearly caused him to be fired.

"To hell with my career," he said. "Let's talk about something really interesting like *your* career. Tell me, Mr. Rattenbury, what happened over there in Canada that forced you to retire from architecture?"

Was this a hallucination? Or had he actually said what I thought he said?

It took a few moments for the full meaning of his words to penetrate, and in the silence that followed I could sense Rats drawing himself up beside me. Needless to say, I drew myself up too. I was stunned. It was as if a protective barrier had been shattered letting in cold and darkness and rain, the barrier that separated servants from their masters. Percy had uttered blasphemy.

Rats pretended he didn't understand or hadn't heard correctly. "Canada?" he said. "I'm afraid you've lost me."

"Surely, you remember," Percy said, his voice cold, sugary sweet. "You tried to get credit for another architect's design, some man who was working for you. But your architectural colleagues over there in Canada found out about it. It must have been very embarrassing."

Percy twisted around to look at Rats, but Rats was looking at me—glaring. Then he turned to Percy.

"Are you trying to provoke me, young man?" he said. "Because if you are, you might very well end up losing your job."

"I'm just trying to keep up my end of the conversation," he said. "You were asking me about my career, well, now I'm asking you about yours. I always wanted to understand how it must have felt to be considered a world-renowned architect one minute and a fraud the next. What an incredible comedown!"

I saw Rats' hands fly up to grab Percy's coat or the back of his neck, I couldn't tell which—it was so sudden—and we swerved sharply to the right, throwing us all forward.

"What are you doing?" I yelled. "What in God's name do you think you're doing? Can't you see he's driving? We're going to crash!"

"Why you ungrateful little—" said Rats.

"I can't believe this is happening!" I said.

"He better not touch me," said Percy. "If he touches me, so help me God, I'll sue him for assault. I'll go to the police. Oh, wouldn't the press love to find out why he assaulted me."

I didn't know what else to do except put my arms around Rats, to restrain him. But he did not attempt to lunge at Percy again. Perhaps he realized he might cause an accident.

The remaining twenty minutes in that dismal car were excruciating, sitting there in the dark silence. How it dragged. How heavy the silence felt. There was nothing to do but listen to the wipers whipping back and forth like the beat of a frantic metronome, contemplate the exhausting scene that had just taken place, and hate myself. Ah yes, I hated myself: for not being able to prevent it and not seeing it coming. How could it all have happened so quickly, coming and going and changing everything before I was aware? I had a frightful, fantastic vision of Rats demanding that I explain, amidst accusations and threats, precisely how Percy had come to know about his Canadian difficulties. All the way back I had this worry which, as it turned out, was completely rational, that when Rats asked me how Percy could have said what he said, he'd trap me into revealing something about my affair with him. Pressed close and sweating, my limbs trembling and my head wobbling like a very old and tired woman, I survived those twenty minutes by trying to imagine what Percy should say to Rats the next day, how he should apologize and try to set things right.

5

I wanted to lay it out calmly, rationally, but knew I wouldn't be able to if he didn't produce at least some mimicry of remorse. So when Percy came to my room later that night and I heard the careless smirk in his voice, I let him have it, all of it, trembling with emotion.

"I cannot believe you said that to Rats. Of all the insinuating, treacherous little—Christ! What were you thinking? Tomorrow, you had better tell him you learned about the Canadian scandal from a shopkeeper in town. Say you forgot who told you. Then you had better tell him you're sorry. Really lay it on. Weep, implore, fall to your knees if you have to."

There was a long silence before he spoke in a pointedly mocking tone: "You can't be serious."

He was lying next to me on top of the covers, still wearing his shirt and trousers, his legs stretched out, his arms folded beneath his head. Even in the darkness, I could see he was smiling; I could sense his amusement in the darkness. He seemed to regard the episode in the car as a form of entertainment. Although this is the very attitude I'd been expecting from him, I was rendered mute by it.

"What?" I said.

"Will you give me a break, Alma? Good Lord! He *deserved* everything I said. The man was asking to be taken down a notch or two. Why is that so hard to understand?"

I pushed myself up to a sitting position and switched on the lamp on my nightstand. "Do you have any idea of the damage you did, Percy?" I said. "Jesus good Christ. It was a cheap, crawling, shabby trick. It was as though you were bragging that you and I are allies, that we talk about him behind his back."

He shrugged and shook his head.

"How can you refuse to apologize? How can you do this to me? To yourself! Don't you understand that he's going to fire you—and that you're destroying everything we have?"

I shoved him. "Well, don't you?"

"Hey," he said. "Take it easy, Alma."

"If you don't apologize to him tomorrow morning, he's going to have you fired and I won't say a word on your behalf. Not a word. Do you understand that? As it is, I'm sure I'd have to beg him. I'd have to tell him you were upset about something, maybe a death in your family, I don't know what, but I'd have to come up with something pretty good. Otherwise, you're gone."

He was like some willfully dense two-year-old who covers his ears and refuses to listen, a fortress of self-centered, stubborn opposition, and I really could have seen him fired without a shadow of remorse. Worse, at that instant, I could have smashed his brains out with the flat side of an axe; I wanted to smash his brains out just to wipe the smile off his face.

Percy, however, saw nothing to be concerned about, and again said he would not apologize. It was a matter of pride, he said.

Which provoked me beyond anger. "You think I'm not serious," I said. "I'll let him fire you and never see you again. I don't want to do that, but I will if you force me. You have no idea how upset I am. And Rats, my God! I'm lucky if he doesn't divorce me. He went to his study without even saying good night. He was trembling. How could you do something like that to him?"

He had a thin cynical smile on his mouth. "I think it's

wonderful how close you two are, how you always come to each other's defense."

"You're such a child, Percy."

"And what are you, deaf?" he said sharply, sitting up straight. "Didn't you hear what he said to me? How can you side with him over me? Don't I mean anything to you?"

"We're not getting anywhere," I said. "Let's just be quiet. I can't take this any longer—"

"Or maybe you just think he can say anything he wants to me because I'm just a chauffeur. I'm supposed to just sit there and smile. All that rot about dignity and pride and my mum, Rats saying he'd throw himself out of a window if he was me. Well, Jesus, Alma, I'm sorry, I just have no idea what I'm supposed to say to something like that."

He was still a moment, as the anger seemed to seep out of him. "Come on, Alma, all I did was give him a little taste of what he was dishing out to me. I didn't mean anything by it, really."

"You don't get it, do you? You didn't just attack him. You hurt me, Percy. When I told you about the difficulties Rats had in Canada, that was in confidence. Has it even occurred to you that you were betraying my trust in you?"

He offered no suggestion of understanding at all. Instead: "What about *you* betraying me?" he said. "Why, you were sitting right there in the car pretending you didn't even notice how he insulted me. The only time you said anything was when you thought he said something insulting to women. How do you think that made me feel? And now, look at you. I know you think I'm nothing more than a ridiculous and impetuous child. I can see it in your face. It's been a waste of time trying to talk to you."

After Percy told me that it was a waste of time trying to talk to me, what was there left for me to say? Nothing. Nothing but,

"Oh, how I wish you would leave me alone," which is what I did say as I rolled over, my back to him, and opened my book. I supposed I could have said something else but imagining him lying there, imagining his knit brows and that peculiar arrogant quality in his eyes, as if he thought he understood something that was just beyond my reach, I knew nothing would come of it, and an immense sorrow came over me. The feeling was followed by a voice—it could have been my mother's, someone I knew intimately, a woman's voice but not my own. It was scolding me, "How could you, a more or less worldly middle-aged woman, a mother no less, have ever thought this boy could be a fit lover for you? What on earth could there be in common between yourself and this seventeen-year-old boy you call Percy? What were you thinking?"

At that moment the full absurdity of the affair sank in, the mistake laid bare.

Desperately, I tried to compose a sentence in my head. Thank you, Percy, it was fun, a wonderful adventure, but now it's over.

I just couldn't say it. I knew too well how I'd hatched the affair, how I'd invited him into bed with me—coaxed him, really—and taken his virginity from him. (I remembered all too well that this was a boy who lost his mother when he was six.) I guess I was too cowardly (and vain and selfish) to admit to myself that I'd harmed him, and would be harming him even more, by continuing the affair. I imagined him lost without me.

My tears softened my bedmate, my lover. He sat up for a moment looking confused, as though not knowing where he was, and then put his arms around me, drawing me close to him, shifting himself onto me.

"Alma, what's going on?" he asked, his voice as mild as milk.

"What's going on?" I repeated his question in a mocking way because I did not want to, indeed could not very well, describe my state of mind without hurting his feelings.

"Why are you crying?"

"Why? How do I know?" I said. "I'm just crying."

"Listen, Alma, maybe I overdid it with Rats back there in the car." Percy's voice had changed. He didn't sound angry anymore. "Maybe I shouldn't have made those comments about what happened with him in Canada. I just wish you'd try to understand what it must have felt like to have him ask me how I could stand being another man's servant. I started thinking about it as I was driving and I thought—if I just sit here and swallow what he's dishing out to me, I *am* his inferior. I'm sorry I said what I said but I wouldn't have if he hadn't insulted me. I wish you'd try to understand that he provoked me, Alma."

I thought he had a point. I reminded myself that he did not intend to hurt me, and that as recently as that afternoon I thought I loved him. But it didn't seem to make a difference, and I just lay there in silence, staring at the center of the ceiling where a braid of plaster flower petals surrounded a crystal light fixture, taking shallow breaths, feeling his weight pressing me into the mattress, feeling more and more uncomfortable with the way he was playing with my fingers, slowly opening and closing the fingers of one of my hands. Had I begun to detest him? No, surely not. It was more that the attributes I once thought attractive—his spontaneity, his fragility, his strangeness, all the ways he needed to be taken care of—had begun to actually feel like burdens. I imagined, wrongly, that being in love with a young man would liberate me. Instead, I had the sense that I was saddled with a screaming, clutching child and could not, no matter what I thought best for myself, disentangle myself.

It was a very bad moment that got worse when I tried to pull away from him, saying, "I need to get up, Percy."

He released me partially but kept his hands clamped on my shoulders and muttered something about how much he loved me, that I was his whole life. Then he lowered himself and began pressing his head against me, rotating his cheek against my breast. My breast actually hurt where he touched me.

"No, Percy, please don't do that," I said.

"Alma, it's only that I want to—"

"I'm not in the mood. I'm not in the *mood!*"

He lay there looking at me, his mouth a thin straight line. Then: "Would you mind telling me what's the matter," he said, still holding me, his touch more restraint than affection.

I yanked free.

"I said I need to get up," I said as I got out of bed, my breasts flopping, and got into my kimono without quite looking at him.

"No, really," he said, "what exactly is bothering you tonight?"

Now I looked at him. "I told you already. I find your behavior incredibly immature."

"Chauffeurs are immature people," he said, not making any sense at all. "Of course, I'm immature. I'm mentally deranged." And he gave himself an enormous open-handed clout against his forehead. "You think I'm sane? Look at this! (clout) I'm completely crazy. (clout, clout) Why else would I be in a position like this? Rats is right. Being somebody's chauffeur is degrading. And I've reached a point where I can't take it any longer. I've got to make a change—to go somewhere where I can have a normal life, a life without dishonor, without lies, dirt. I feel as if it's strangling me. Honestly, Alma, if I don't get out of here soon, I think I really will throw myself from a window."

He was expecting me to respond but I didn't. I had moved over to my dressing table on the other side of the room and sat in front of the mirror. I looked exhausted. Even in the dim light I could see the bags under my eyes.

"Did you hear me?" he said. "I'm talking about quitting."

"I heard," I said and began brushing my hair.

He descended from the bed and stood in the middle of the room, hands sunk in his pockets, staring at me from behind, and then came over to the dressing table. "Okay, you heard. Now tell me what do you think?"

"It's ridiculous. That's what I think."

"Why is it ridiculous?"

"You have nowhere to go, Percy."

"There's London," he said, kneeling and putting his arms around my waist. In the mirror, I could see his arms and hands and some of his hair, but none of his face. I looked like I had two sets of arms.

"I could go to London," he said. "What do you say to going to London with me?" He paused dramatically, drawing himself erect, his large eyes now blinking at me in the mirror, as an exultant tone began to find its way into his words. "There are all sorts of jobs there, and I could go to school at night—why couldn't I? I really do think Rats was right about that. I should go to night school and learn some new skills. Other people do and find good jobs, so why can't I? It might be a struggle for a while, but at least I could have some dignity in my life—*we* could have some dignity."

"You want to go to London, fine. But please don't include me."

"Why can't we go together? We have to be together," he said. "I'd never go without you. Never."

"That's nonsense."

"It's not nonsense. I'm serious."

I turned my head slowly to look at him. Then I resumed brushing my hair. "No, it's not nonsense?" I said. "Well, what about Felix? I have a six-year-old son in case you forgot."

"We can take him with us."

I remember ordering myself to take deep breaths, to stay calm. I really disliked him at that moment. I remember how blank and stupid his face looked, with his eyes wide open, his lips stretched to a funny little smile of triumph. His lips were—I think this is the only word for what they were doing—smirking.

"Are you trying to be funny?" I said.

"I'm not trying to be anything. I'm talking about a plan for our future, a way to build a life for ourselves."

"Ha!" I said, not looking at him, still brushing my hair.

"It's the money, isn't? You're worried about the money."

"Money? Why would I worry about money if we ran away to London? Just because I have a little boy, and neither of us has a job, and we wouldn't even have a place to live?"

He gave forth a small sigh of exasperation.

I did not look at him; I continued brushing my hair.

"You know, you don't give me much credit, Alma. And you never consider how I feel. Just put yourself in my place. I'm a servant here, a man who is at your husband's beck and call at any time on any day. Do you think it's pleasant knowing that I'm my lover's employee? I never get to go to a party with you. How do you think I feel when I drop you off at a friend's house, at a reception, and you're having a great time without me—"

"I've always had the impression that you loathe my friends. You always poke fun at them—"

"May I finish?" he said. "I'm telling you something you really need to hear. Goddamn it. You'll sleep with me but you won't go to a party with me. It's all right for you to go to a party and have a great time but I have to wait in the car. It's simply not fair. I mean, how could I—how could anyone—have self-respect in that position? It's insupportable. It has become insupportable."

"Where are you going with this?"

"Alma," he said, the broken note in his voice making me wince, "if we had our own place in London and I had a regular job, everything would be different. I could begin to feel like a normal person. And we'd be together, maybe one day even get married. Go the whole circuit. You know, me Tarzan, you Jane."

"Percy, honey . . ." I said.

"Yes?"

"I'm already married."

"Oh, you are? Great response, Alma. Thank you for the information."

I had stopped brushing my hair and let my arms fall to my side. Now I felt sad—sad rather than angry.

"Don't you think we're entitled to live like a normal couple?" he said.

"Yes, I suppose," I said, guilt sweeping over me for arguing with this boy whom I purported to love, for wishing he would just go to London if that's what he wanted instead of sitting there indicting me. And as usual, when there was disagreement between us, I felt I was the one at fault. "I just don't know, Percy. I don't know. I'm sorry. For you. For me. I just don't know."

"We can make it," he said. "We'll be okay."

"We'll be okay?" I said. "How could we possibly be okay?"

"All I know is I love you, Alma," he said. "I love you so much."

"Percy, that's enough . . . please."

"Enough of what? What are you saying?"

"It's madness, that's what I'm saying. And I'd like to get some rest."

"I know I can't offer you much, Alma. All I have to offer is myself and that I love you more than anything on earth."

He was being so naïve and sentimental and arrogant that I ought to have told him, You're right, you can't offer me much, and now, if you don't mind, would you please either shut up and go to sleep or leave me alone and go back to your room. Instead, as usual, I put my arms around him to comfort him, to tell him everything would be fine. And in spite of our fight, in spite of my realization that our affair was absurd and that I was deeply, painfully weary of him and not feeling in the least desirous, we climbed into bed and made love.

6

Why do I give in so easily? Do I really think Percy, or any man, has the right to do to me whatever he wants?

The question baffles me, but I will table it for now and instead turn my attention to my encounter with Rats the next morning—not because it portrays me in a more positive light, but because I honestly have no idea why I began sleeping with Percy and why I couldn't stop. I only wanted to make him happy. I meant well. Which, I know, is not any kind of explanation.

In any case, the next morning I was lying on my bed reading a book—I had acquired the habit of reading in bed till Felix jumped on top of me and pulled me out—when I heard Rats' heavy tread coming down the hall, and then a knock.

"Alma," he said through the crack in the door, and after a moment, moved into sight. I noticed that he looked tired and hadn't shaved evenly: his cheeks were smooth but there was stubble on the sides of his chin. "May I sit here?" he asked, touching his fingertips to the bed, his voice icily polite, and then adding with what sounded to me like a hint of irony, "Or would that make you uncomfortable?"

He never visited my bedroom, he hardly spoke to me at all, but I had known he might visit that morning. I knew he might want to confer about the incident in the car, and I imagined myself calm, very lucid and ready. I'd been preparing myself.

Yet his actual presence on the bed made me quite uncomfortable.

I groped for my kimono and tried to slip into it without appearing hurried, as he silently watched. I was not frightened. I simply felt mortified, and perhaps he picked it up or saw it on my face, for after staring at me a moment, he shifted his weight against the cushions, and spoke in his most stilted voice: "My dear, Alma, I must apologize for barging in on you in this way, but I didn't know when you'd be coming down, and so I thought—"

He stopped short, catching sight of Felix, who had been playing in his room across the hall, and had now run into my bedroom, this six-year-old mass of energy tripping on his long blue robe, circling the room and then throwing himself into my arms. Felix wanted to know if I could help him find one of his toys. I asked where he had seen it last, but Rats rubbed his upper lip and gave him a stern look. "What the deuce do you mean interrupting us like this?" he said sharply and told him to get Irene to help.

If Rats had the ability to read other people's feelings, he would have noted the shrinking, bewildered look that the boy gave first to me and then to his father. But he did not have that ability, and he did not see anything. I put my face near Felix's and whispered, "I'll help you find it later, as soon as Daddy and I finish talking," and then kissed him on the cheek and gave him a gentle shove toward the door.

"Sorry," I said to Rats. "What were you saying?"

He tried to complete his thought. "I've made a decision . . ."

Here it comes, I thought.

"I think it would be best if we let Percy go."

"Oh?" I said, my voice soft, indifferent, deliberately devoid of inflection. "Fire him?"

"Precisely."

"And why?"

His eyebrows arched. "You know perfectly well."

"I don't," I said, shrugging my shoulders and trying to produce a bored, dismissive smile. "I really don't."

"Isn't it obvious?"

"Why are you being coy?" I said. "Why don't you just tell me what's on your mind?"

"What took place in the car . . ."

"Yes?"

"His behavior toward me last night in the car, it was completely out of line, wouldn't you agree?"

"Of course, I agree. It was completely out of line," I said quickly and firmly, looking him straight in the eyes, no longer trying to appear dispassionate, and then added with a note of sarcasm: "But fire him? Aren't we overreacting just a trifle, Rats?"

"There is a right way to behave and there is a wrong way, and that was definitely the wrong way—"

"Of course it was the wrong way. I couldn't agree more, darling. It's just that I think the punishment should fit the crime." I paused here. "Maybe you should also consider, Rats, that Percy might have been reacting to you. You do remember, don't you, telling him you'd jump out of a window if you were he? That was a bit insensitive of you, don't you think?"

There was a silence, and then he almost seemed to lose his mind with indignation.

"I can hardly *believe* that instead of holding Percy responsible for his misbehavior you can sit there and say that I, the person he attacked, is the one who is actually to blame. You heard what he said. You know the way he acts. Yet you're always so quick to let me know what my insufficiencies are"—he was speaking in a rush—"forgetting that I keep him here only because of you, in order for you to have a chauffeur of your own, which seems to mean so much to you. You came to me and said, Rats, I need a chauffeur for my appointments. I believed you. I didn't ask any questions. I gave him to you." Rats held up his hands here the way he did when he thought I was about to raise an objection so meaningless it didn't deserve to be spoken. "Jesus, Alma, I've given everything to you—my heart and my soul, and now I find out that my kindness has been used against me and the two of you have been behaving improperly."

The word "improperly" was said softly but I felt it like a kick. Did he know? It was a possibility that I had been considering for quite a while. But I still couldn't believe it. Had he been holding his tongue, hoping, perhaps, to avoid a scandal? If that was true, when had he noticed it? During the drive yesterday? Or earlier? Did this mean, could this possibly mean, he knows everything? I was greatly tempted that morning to put an end to these speculations and ask Rats, directly, if he believed I was having an affair with Percy. But I did not yield to the temptation. Besides being a reasonably intelligent woman, I'm a practical one and knew that I would have to weigh my words if I wanted to keep both my marriage and my chauffeur. But weigh my words how? I had no idea—none except to deny every accusation, and to act hurt and indignant.

"Rats! You sit there and say that—to me!"

I waited for him to answer, but he was silent, looking away from me, a proud stern look on his face.

"Why won't you answer me?" I said. "What's the matter with you? I detest the way you're insinuating."

"I'm not insinuating. And nothing's the matter with me."

"I can't think of anything more despicable than someone making a vague innuendo about my propriety. I shall never forgive you. Would you be so kind as to tell me how you can accuse me of behaving improperly?"

Rats gave a sly smile. "Because, darling, you have."

"This is so tiresome. How?"

He looked at me in silence, in an impatient manner. "All right, yesterday evening in the car he said things to me about my affairs in Canada. Where could he have learned about them if not from you?" He shrugged his shoulders slightly and turned away, as if he considered the matter closed.

"Now see here, Rats," I exclaimed, "there's a false assumption you're making, and that is that I'm the only person in England familiar with the details of your career and therefore the only person who could have told him about Canada."

"On the contrary, my dear, I know for a fact that you are the only one."

"Did you hear me tell him? Has someone told you I did?"

"No."

"Then how can you say it?"

He remained silent.

"You know, Rats, there's a definite grudging, spiteful streak in your character, and I really don't like it."

"My character is not at issue."

I shook my head slightly, as though I couldn't believe how stupid I was. "Oh, pardon me, I forgot, it's my character that's at issue."

"Well, did you tell him or didn't you?"

"What if I said I didn't? Would you believe me?"

For a moment he sat quite still on the bed, his thick eyebrows beetling, his jaw trembling a little, his eyes toward the window. "No," he declared at last, turning his head to look at me, "I wouldn't."

"What I don't understand is why in God's name, if you've already made your mind up, you bother to ask me at all?"

"I want to hear you say it."

"Say what? Say we spend all our time gossiping about you? Would that make you happy?"

"No," he shook his head back and forth; his face had become softer, almost gentle. His voice sank to a hoarse whisper. "No, it would not make me happy."

"For pity's sake, Rats, don't let's continue like this. It can't do either of us any good. It's time to stop torturing ourselves about Canada. Canada is over. We're in England now. And as for me gossiping about you with Percy, I'd sooner cut my leg off. Why would I lie about such a thing?"

Rats gave another sly smile. "To protect him."

"*What?* Protect Percy? Are you serious? He means nothing to me. If you think otherwise, then you don't know the least thing about me. I have no idea where he learned about Canada. Can't you possibly understand a thing as simple as that?" I moved my head close to him and began hollering right into his face. "Let me tell you, once and for all: go ahead and fire him if you really must. I won't try to stop you. But if you fire him because you want to get back at me or because you think I've been disloyal to you with him, you'd be making a hideous mistake."

I had meant to intimidate him, or at the very least to put him on the defensive, but now saw that Rats' anger and suspicion, far from retreating, were actually gathering strength and growing bolder, like a river about to overflow a dam. I looked at his pink face, now flushed with excitement, framed in the light from the window, white hair that had never seemed so white, and I was suddenly convinced that my worst fears were correct: yes, my marriage was in jeopardy; yes, Rats wanted to hurt me—to retaliate against me. If he had hackles, they'd be raised. At the same time, I noticed that his hand, his hand that had been clasped on his lap a moment ago, his large hand with the powerful knotty knuckles and bulging veins, had moved on top of mine. Not an affectionate move.

I dared not risk the slightest movement of my hand, not the slightest twitch, for fear any resistance might rouse my adversary. And I was right, for when I at last tried to quietly withdraw my hand from his, he enclosed it as if he had captured an animal in a trap, the gesture so sudden and despotic, and so uncharacteristic, that all I could do was raise my eyes and stare at him.

"We're not talking about *my* mistakes," he said in a high, trembling growl. "Everybody who knows me knows I've been a good husband. Have I ever denied you anything since we've been married?"

"Rats! I never said you had!"

"Will you look me in the face and swear to me you did not tell Percy about my Canadian difficulties?"

"I told you, I didn't."

"Have you never told anybody in Bournemouth—or anywhere else—that I had once been accused of fraud? Answer me that!"

"I don't understand how you can talk to me like this, as though you were my enemy?"

"I'm not your enemy, but you're mine!"

"How can you say that, Rats? I love you."

"You call this love, a wife who talks about her husband to the servants"—his voice made an odd little click—"it's hatred, not love. You hate me."

"How absurd—because you think I spoke to Percy about you?"

"Because of everything," he said. "The way you speak about me, the way you speak *to* me, the way you react when we touch. Everything. The way you're all closed up. You're like a wall to me. Last winter you even insisted on sleeping in a separate bedroom."

"Ah, so that's what's behind all this," I exclaimed. "You're not cross with me still, are you, for wanting to change bedrooms?"

"Cross!" he said, and made an expression so bewildered, so

abject, that for one second I was moved to pity, then the next drawn back to absolute revulsion. "Good Lord! Cross is what a husband feels when his wife refuses to laugh at one of his jokes. My wife refuses to sleep with me!"

I flung my hands up in exasperation. "Is this whole thing about you wanting me to confess something I said to Percy or is it about you wanting me to allow you to move back into my bed? I should really appreciate knowing. What *do* you want from me?"

"I . . ." he whispered, reaching a hand to touch my hair. "I just want . . ."

"What, dear, what do you want?"

Color suddenly seeped back into his face, giving him a queer dark look.

"Yes, Rats?"

"I just want you to sleep with me again!" He pounded the mattress with his fist so hard that my book bounced and fell to the floor.

I stared at him, speechless. Now this was the one thing I never thought he'd say—what he had not said since the day he moved out of our bedroom—the one thing I couldn't argue.

"That's what I *want,* as if you cared."

"How can you say such a thing? Of course I care, darling. You know I do."

"Then sleep with me."

"Rats, when have I ever refused?"

"Sleep with me now."

Upstairs, in the attic apartment, there was the sound of someone walking, the creaking of floorboards, and I found myself suddenly worrying that Percy might come to my door, that he might see me on the bed with Rats. I knew exactly how many steps there are from the attic to the second floor, how many steps it took Percy to move through the hall into my room.

The creaking grew louder and louder, and I sat very still, listening. It almost obscured the smaller, but unmistakable sound of Rats' breathing, the hard rasp of air entering and exiting his nostrils.

"This very moment?"

"Yes, why not?"

"There's no need to be precipitous."

"Yes, there is . . . I've never in my life felt a greater need to be precipitous."

"And you've had some precipitous needs in your time, haven't you, darling?"

"If you mock me, Alma, then you've proved my point."

"Which point is that?"

"Oh. I don't know. I really don't care. Let's do it. Let's just do it—please—"

I sat there a moment looking at Rats' upper lip, at the pink flesh cleft by a vertical wrinkle that divided his upper lip in two, and at his short straight eyelashes. I could not believe that sexual relations could possibly take place, that it would come down to that, but on the other hand I did not see what else I could do. In hindsight, I could have made an excuse, told him I had a headache or my monthlies or something of that sort. Instead, feeling for the moment at a complete loss, feeling that if I didn't go along my marriage would end—that my home, my family, everything that I loved would dissolve like steam into thin air—I leaned forward and opened my arms to him, and said, "Well, then, if that's what you really want, come along, let's get started, shall we?"

That must have sounded rather cold, as though I were a prostitute offering services, for he did not move, and after looking at me for a moment, asked: "Alma, what do you have against me?"

"What a question! How can you ask something like that? I love you."

"Tell me the truth . . . tell it once and for all. You really don't like me very much, do you?"

"I told you the truth. I love you."

"Listen, I won't blame you if you don't want to make love with me—look at me. I'm an old man, and with a harelip too. I'll understand."

"I want whatever you want," I said.

"Are you absolutely sure?"

"Yes."

I was lying, of course. And anyone with eyes in their head would have known I was lying—except for Rats. He had no idea. He was always ready to hope, even when there was no hope, and so he moved into my arms, suddenly his mouth on mine, emphatic, insistent, his tongue pushing into my mouth, as though he were avenging himself on my mouth for all the nights I slept without him. The next moment he was pressing his loins against me as though fixing his seal to an official document, his arms like vices wrapping around me, fingers curling around my arm so tightly that I thought they'd leave bruises. This will soon be over, I said to myself, as I sank back onto the bed, shivering with grief and disgust, remembering all the times he had taken my breasts in his hands and squeezed till they almost hurt, all the times he had taken my hair in his fingers, his fingers like those of a coal miner, and pinned my skull to the mattress, and all the times I had promised myself that I would never again, for the sake of expediency, allow him to do to me what he was now doing.

I could hear Felix playing in the hall outside my door, and I squirmed a little, trying to free myself from his enormous fingers that had found their way inside my kimono and were now twisting my nipples. He must have heard Felix too because he suddenly got to his feet and closed the bedroom door, turning the lock. When he returned to the bed, I noticed that his belt was unbuckled and his trousers were unzipped.

"Please, Rats, I'd rather not," I begged.

He looked at me incredulously, with something like shocked amusement. "What the devil!"

"I'm saying I'd rather not, if you don't mind."

"What is it?"

"Rats, I'm sorry darling, but I'm not feeling well."

"Don't be ridiculous, Alma. You're acting like a cock tease. You already told me I could."

"Rats, I'd like you to go now."

"You can't suddenly change your mind in the middle, Alma. Not after you told me I could do it. I'm all excited now. I can't stop now."

He pushed me back on the bed, spread-eagling himself over me, his left hand trying to push apart my legs, as his right grabbed hold of my breast.

"Rats, what are you doing?"

"Hold still!"

"I told you I'm feeling sick."

"Don't fight it, Alma. Just go with it."

"I'm begging you, Rats. Stop it!"

I twisted my knees together like a pretzel so he couldn't open me up; I squirmed when he tried to insert himself into me.

"For God's sakes, Alma, I can't do it if you don't give me a little cooperation. You're ruining everything. If you would just cooperate we'd be done in a minute."

"Rats, get off me! I'm sick, I'm telling you!"

What should I have done? Flail at him? Scream? Call out for help? But then, as though realizing, at last, that I wouldn't— couldn't—do anything, that I was helpless, I broke into sobs. The sobs came in rapid little breaths, and they began coming faster and faster, gaining momentum like a wave.

Rats had a blind spot. The blind spot was my hysteria. He suddenly lifted himself off me, fearing, correctly, that I was on the verge of losing control. My sobbing really seemed to frighten him. As long as I remained fairly rigid and inexpressive during sex, Rats was quite comfortable doing to me whatever he wanted. But now he looked pitiful. He was shaking his head from side to side, pulling up his trousers, tucking in his shirt, buckling his belt, smoothing his waistcoat, straightening his tie, looking quite aghast. "Sorry about that. I'm really sorry that you should have been exposed to that." (That's the word he used, "exposed.")

"Rats, have you gone mad!" My voice came out clipped and hard, as more tears came to my eyes. "What did you do that for? How on earth could you behave like that with me? What's wrong with you?"

He raised his finger to my lips, silencing me. Then I felt his hand on my cheek and heard him stammer: "I don't know what got into me."

I was crying in earnest once again, a long shrill sound coming out of my mouth that threatened to go on and on.

He clasped his hands, a prayerful gesture. "All right," he said low and even. "All right." His voice was calm, soothing, as if he were trying to reassure a spooked horse. "All right," he said again, and begged my pardon for the attempted rape—he called it "rudeness."

"I wish you'd go now. To do such a thing to me, to *me*, to *me!*"

"Please believe—"

I felt ashamed for him and *of* him, this large familiar man sitting on the edge of my bed, this man who had often been so sweet to me and was now begging my forgiveness.

"Don't worry about it, Alma. We'll just go on as if . . . I never came to visit you this morning. Please, Alma, why don't we just forget everything."

Suddenly my tears stopped. I asked him what he was trying to say, what he intended by saying, "Why don't we just forget everything?"

Rats lowered his eyes, as if he were too embarrassed to explain.

"We'll forget *what?*" I asked. "What will we forget?"

He looked perplexed, uncomprehending, and then said something perplexing and incomprehensible, "*Mon cher, je suis un homme* who will do anything for peace."

I had been shocked by his brutality and crudeness, but now I was listening.

"Shall we forget I visited you this morning?" he said. "Can we just forget we even saw each other?"

I said I'd very much like to forget I saw him this morning and I'd also very much like to forget that Canada had been introduced into the conversation yesterday in the car.

"Yes, if that's what you want."

"Agreed."

He nodded solemnly.

"And Percy," I asked, despising myself for turning his violence to my advantage, "what will you do with him?"

"You decide."

I looked at him, searched his face, feeling a pang of worry that this sharp-nosed fox, this sham innocent who had pounced on me and let me go, was once again preparing to pounce. "You're very sly," I said. "Because if Percy is rude to you again, you can say I'm responsible."

"What! That's nonsense."

"You'll say I'm protecting him."

"I won't. I'm giving you my word."

My first instinct was to tell him to go ahead and fire Percy since that was what he said he wanted. If I told him to keep Percy it would mean that my affection for our chauffeur was so strong that I could disregard the fact that he had been impossibly rude to my husband who had just a moment ago expressed an unequivocal desire to fire him. I didn't want to give Rats the satisfaction of proving he was right about Percy and me. I wanted to defeat Rats but I wanted to keep Percy more.

"Don't forget then," I said, "you insisted that I decide."

"Of course."

"All right, I agree that Percy hurt your feelings. But I don't believe he did it on purpose. So I think that if he really is, well, quite remorseful and promises never to speak to you in that tone again, you could give him a second chance. If he's the sort of boy I imagine, he's probably realized his mistake already. You yourself, in any case, have always said to me that you believe in second chances."

"Yes," he said, with sudden solemnity. "I have always said I believe in second chances."

"I think we should keep Percy on staff for your sake as well, in order that you may change your opinion of me. You—I don't know why—think I've been disloyal to you in some way with Percy. Well, you're mistaken. I'm not that sort of wife! And I can only prove that to you if we keep Percy on staff."

"Yes," he said again with solemnity, accepting my terms because he felt he deserved my resentment, deserved to be punished. "I see your point. With Percy on staff I'll have a chance to change my mind about you."

Such then was the bargain we struck. Rats pledged to tolerate Percy's presence in our home not because he trusted me, but because he let me blackmail him, and in letting me blackmail him, proved his suspicions of Percy and me correct.

7

Which may explain why, during the days that followed, Rats seemed compelled to take revenge on Percy by forcing him to do a lot of meaningless, abasing, make-work kinds of tasks, the sort of thing one might expect from a fairy-tale potentate bent on demonstrating his unrestricted power.

One afternoon, for example, perhaps a week after Rats' "rudeness," he came into the garden while I was planting bulbs and Percy was painting the fence.

"Who told you to paint the fence?" Rats asked.

Percy told him he had.

"Didn't I tell you to scrape and sand the wood first?"

"I scraped and sanded already."

"You scraped and sanded *already?* Does this look scraped and sanded to you?" He ran his fingers along the edge of a board. There were spots of paint in the grooves and in the knots of the wood.

I said, "It looks good enough to me."

"I'm asking Percy, darling," Rats told me.

"Well, it does."

Percy said it looked good enough to him, too.

"Run your finger along here," he said, and lifted Percy's finger to the board. "Does this feel smooth to you?"

Percy didn't answer.

"Rats," I said.

He asked Percy again if the board was smooth. Percy said no, it didn't feel smooth.

"Don't put fresh paint on wood until you've first sanded away the old." He handed Percy some sandpaper. Percy began sanding while Rats watched, making comments. "The trouble with you, Percy," he said, "is that you think other people are stupid. You think that when you do a second-rate job nobody will notice. You want to take the easy way."

In bed later that night, Percy and I talked about Rats. How he would stay up late playing with his Egyptian slave figurines. How he lined them up in columns according to height, how he had once told me that my eyes had a "bewitching" tendency to change color in different lights, and not suspecting Percy would take this to heart, I told him how Rats used to make love to me, how he raced and heaved, then his bent knees extended like a spring and he was done. Only one minute required. How efficient he was! I also told him how Rats tried to force himself on me the other morning.

Forever after, I dream of reliving that evening and taking those words back. But I can't. Nor did Percy hesitate; all he did was stare and say, "The man doesn't deserve to live."

8

As for my relationship with Rats, after the blackmail that culminated in my getting to keep Percy, he treated me as if nothing happened. He still gave me compliments. If anything, they were less outlandish and inappropriate than before, although nothing that would be confused with genuine affection. He didn't refer to the incident in the car again nor did I refer to his "rudeness" in my bedroom.

If there was any change in my attitude toward him, you might say there was a heightened watchfulness. I watched to see if he was watching me, but when I concluded he wasn't, I returned to normal.

I did not quite return to normal with Percy, however. Indeed, things became rather more strained and complicated between the two of us. I believed that since Rats now suspected us, it was inevitable that one day, by accident or on purpose, we'd get caught. It was a certainty. Which made me a little too tense to have sex, although we kept right on sleeping together, though that was all we did—sleep—him on his side of the bed, and me on mine. We also stopped seeing each other as often during the day. Far off indeed were the days when I used to smile whenever I glanced at him, when I would imagine him the most fascinating seventeen-year-old I had ever met. The fight we had ruined that. Suddenly, palpably, Percy actually seemed to lose, in my eyes, his substance as a person. I lost all interest in his conversation. I also lost a sense of our rightness, the conviction that what we had to offer each other was worth all the deceit and manipulation required to keep our affair alive. How quickly everything changed! True, every now and then we rolled into each other's arms in bed. Most of the time, however, I felt toward him an obscure and almost unrelenting impatience.

My life, in short, after the incident in the car, seemed to settle into a rather tense, vigilant routine, almost wholly lacking in drama.

Unfortunately, the routine period didn't last. All of a sudden, everything became quite dramatic again.

I was sitting at my dressing table one morning, precisely thirteen days after the car incident, when I noticed a distinct soreness in my breasts, a sensitivity that was different yet vaguely familiar. My stomach was feeling odd, too, a bit queasy. I sat still for quite a few minutes, my attention on my stomach, waiting for the queasiness to pass. It didn't pass; it got worse. I tried to decide what it might mean. I must have the flu, I thought. Then, slowly, it came to me that people with the flu don't feel sore in their breasts. They feel sore in their joints.

I took off my top and peered in the mirror. My breasts were swollen. I saw it quite clearly. Sitting in front of the mirror with my top off, staring like an idiot for ten, twenty seconds, I saw the connection. It fit. Everything fit. The nausea. The swollen breasts. And last but not least, the period that had not yet arrived, that was already a week late.

Dear God, I'm pregnant.

It can't be true, I told myself. Without a medical examine it's nothing more than speculation.

Which made not the slightest difference to me. I knew, as would any other woman in my situation, that I was pregnant with Percy's baby. Just look at my breasts! And with morning sickness too!

I must think this through, I said to myself. More important, I must compose myself. Take it gently, old girl. Whatever you do, do it calmly. There's too much at stake. It wasn't simply that I was nearly forty and couldn't imagine assuming responsibility—absolute responsibility—for another human life. It was that I was pregnant with my chauffeur's child. There was something fundamentally astonishing about the idea.

What would my friends think? More to the point, what would Rats think? Already I could see the contempt and loathing in his eyes, his lips losing color and trembling. When he found out (which seemed inevitable) my marriage would be over, I'd lose Felix and I'd be tossed out onto the street. The offense was so grave as to preclude even the possibility of forgiveness.

Going to our physician was out of the question, obviously. Even if I could be sure he wouldn't tell Rats, which I wasn't, there was a risk in going to his offices: I might be recognized in his waiting room by one of his other patients.

God help me!

I pressed my hands against the window and looked at the medley of bright multicolored trees quivering in the wind, the leaves blowing out of them, the pale yellow sun shining through the leaves like a face in the sky. The sun. The sky. The flying leaves. The great wide world. How beautiful it all was! Lord, how lovely! I once was, in every sense of the words, a happy woman. I thought I had everything.

Alas, that was thirteen days ago.

I dressed and walked out into the garden and through the wrought-iron gateway and then down the gravel path that led across the field to the ocean. The water near the beach was all waves, waves of blue and white riding on top of each other, welling up high and breaking into plumes of spray. Wandering through the light salt spray, I couldn't feel my feet touching the sand. I couldn't feel anything, my mind a total blank except for the panic gnawing and scratching inside my skull. I was all nervous energy, mad with it. I wanted to dash about in a dithering maze. But ladies never run, I told myself. Ladies, especially pregnant ladies, walk slowly. No running or jumping, no horseback riding or standing on your head, when pregnant. Or you risk losing the cargo.

Do you want to lose your cargo?

I had wandered to a cove hidden from the rest of the beach by a wall of grassy dune. The coarse grass seemed to lift and fall with the wind as another thought came into my head:

You're not the first woman in the history of the world who needed to abort her pregnancy, now are you?

I eased myself down onto the sand, knelt for a moment, my heart thumping in my chest, and dropped backwards. The air smelled like salt . . . sea air. I lay there breathing it in, staring upwards into the sky, feeling chilled by the cold damp sand.

Sand is always cold in the fall, I thought, a reminder, like a reassurance, that the world would go on. It would stay the same familiar world, and I would stay the same familiar Alma. That was the thought to hold onto. The doctor would remove the tissue from my body and I would get up and get dressed and go on with my life as though nothing had happened.

Well, what else can I do?

I lay on the sand for what might have been an hour, shivering with cold and excitement and fear, staring into the vastness above, at the gulls writing calligraphy in the blue sky, soaring and diving. Other women have abortions all the time, I told myself, so why not me?

It would probably hurt a great deal. It would not, of course, be a walk in the park. It was illegal and immoral. And you had to know how to find a willing physician, one who was competent and confidential. I had a nasty feeling it wouldn't be at all easy to find one. I would probably need assistance. I went over in my head how my bridge "friends" would react. They would be intrigued and would want to hear all about it, but I doubted any would know how to contact an abortionist. Besides, if I told one, they would tell all, and soon everyone would know, and eventually it would get back to Rats.

So I decided to tell Percy.

I went back to the house and looked in the garage, and then the tool shed and his room in the attic. Then I walked around the garden, shouting, "Percy! Where are you, Percy?"

"Over here," he answered.

"Where?"

"Over here."

He was between a hedge and the brick wall reading a book about archeological expeditions in Mexico. That's how Percy spent his time when not driving. Reading and hiding—hiding from Rats.

"Well, Alma," Percy said affectionately, looking up at me from his book. "How are things with you?"

I was struck by the sweetness of his face, half-hidden behind his book, only the top half exposed. How sweet his eyes are! And for a second, I felt a pang at having to share something so sleazy.

"Alma, what's the matter?"

I told him to meet me at the car, and waited till we started and were on the road.

His skin went white and he jerked forward, stunned. "Pregnant?" he said. "How can you be pregnant?"

"You remember we've been having intercourse? You do remember that, don't you?"

"You can't be serious. Are you sure?"

"I thought you would say that. That's what the man always says."

"Well, *are* you sure?"

"Yes," I said.

"Have you seen a doctor?"

"No."

"Then how can you be sure?"

"I have been pregnant before, you know. It's really not very difficult to figure out."

"Listen, Alma, I'm not saying you don't know what you're talking about, but how can you be sure you're pregnant when you haven't seen a doctor?"

"Pull up here," I said, unbuttoning my sweater.

He made a left at Colby Hospital and pulled into the parking lot, to the rear of the four-story building, and then twisted his head around.

"Take a look at this," I said, exposing my breast.

Percy raised his brows and looked back at me, amused. "What's wrong with your breast?"

"Doesn't it look bigger to you?"

"It does look bigger, Alma."

"It looks like a melon."

Percy leaned forward over the seat till his nose was almost touching my breast.

"Feel it," I said. "Put your hand on it. There, how does it feel?"

"Feels larger," he said. "Good God! It really does feel larger."

"Right, Percy, it's puffed up. I'm pregnant. A pregnant woman's breasts have a look all their own. Did you know that?"

Percy stared at my breast. "I can't believe it, I just can't believe it," he said slowly. "Does it hurt?"

"No, not really."

"Jesus."

"Look," I said, buttoning my sweater, "we don't have to talk about this right now."

"Jesus," he said again. "I'm positively numb. I don't know what to say."

"Why don't we just drive?"

"Where do you want to go?"

"I don't care."

He drove around the fringe of Bournemouth and after a while turned into a narrow bumpy lane and started jabbering: "Well, this *is* something . . . it's unbelievable. The news—and it's great . . . great news."

"Percy, what are you talking about? Great news? How could you possibly call this great news?"

"Isn't that what you're supposed to say when a woman tells you she's pregnant? You know, congratulations, I'm happy for you, great news, that sort of thing. It's supposed to be a good thing, isn't it? Everybody is supposed to have at least two babies. It's a moral duty. You're familiar with the Bible, aren't you?"

I wondered whether this should make me angry, but then decided that there was no need; in fact I was faintly relieved to hear him joke. In a way it was refreshing to hear someone speak lightly upon this subject. I leaned forward and touched his neck.

Now he was actually smirking. "And God said to Adam, and to Noah. Be fruitful and multiply, and replenish the earth—"

"You know, of course, I can't keep it."

"What's that?" He was looking at me through the rearview mirror.

"I said, I can't keep it."

"What do you mean—you can't keep it?"

"Oh, Percy."

"What do you mean you can't keep it? I'm really sorry, I just don't know what you're talking about."

"What I've decided," I said, "is to get rid of it."

"Get rid of it, as in abortion?"

"Get rid of it, as in abortion."

"You're not going to let nature take its course?"

"No, I'm not."

"You don't think it might be nice for us to have a baby of our own?"

"No, I don't."

"Isn't abortion illegal?"

"It is illegal. Of course it is."

"So how can you have an abortion, Alma? I mean, what's a nice woman like you doing talking about abortion? What about prison, isn't that a concern?"

I didn't smile or say anything. I tried to collect myself. I breathed, paused. Then I said softly: "You're not helping."

"I'm sorry. I don't mean to make it any worse. I just can't believe you'd consider something so . . . so extreme. Wildly extreme. Really, Alma, I don't know how you can be so cold-blooded about it."

"So you think I'm cold-blooded? You disapprove?"

"I'm sorry, Alma. I didn't mean it that way. I know what you must be feeling."

"I seriously doubt that. I doubt you have any idea what I'm feeling."

"I'm sorry. It's just that we're not talking about getting rid of a wart, you know, we're talking about a baby, a human being." Then he started singing, very loudly, to the tune of "O Tannenbaum," "O human being, O human being, we never shall abort you—"

"Percy?"

"Yes."

"No more singing."

"Sorry."

"Another thing."

"Yes?"

"You keep saying I'm sorry. I wish you'd quit that."

He scratched his head, sighed, and then feigned a cough to

keep from having to speak.

Be patient, I admonished myself. Try to imagine how you'd feel if you were only seventeen and your lover said she intended to abort her pregnancy. But it occurred to me that I didn't have the vaguest idea how a seventeen-year-old boy would *not* want his lover to abort her pregnancy. So I tried as best I could to counterfeit the appearance of understanding.

"I know this must be a lot for you," I said. "I know this is pretty unexpected."

He said the whole thing was too awful to think about. It gave him the creeps, he said, and, then, astonishingly: "I think part of my problem with abortion has to do with losing my mother when I was little . . . you know, the idea that I'd be losing my first child too—"

"Stop it!"

"I'm sorry." His face took on a pained and puzzled look, and he put his hand over his mouth. "Oops."

"How *dare* you," I cried. My body went rigid, absolutely stiff with fury, and I ordered him to stop the car.

He swerved abruptly, throwing me off balance, and brought the car to a halt beside a line of golden beeches, near the summit of a hill; below, pasture and bean fields were spread out like huge carpets.

"What are you doing now?" he asked.

I told him to get out of the car and walk home. I said I'd drive the car home on my own.

"Are you crazy!" he said and didn't get out.

"Get out!"

"You're behaving like a perfect idiot, Alma. And anyway, you've forgotten Irene has to go to the market, and I have to drive her."

I got out and opened his door. I stood over him with my fists on my hips, "Go on, get out of there." Then I grabbed him by the arm and yanked.

"Jesus, take it easy, will you?" Tears trickled out of his eyes.

"Are you going to stop acting like a judgmental bastard?"

"Please, Alma—" He opened the door and got out, and brought his face close to mine. "I didn't mean to sound judgmental. I didn't. Truly I didn't. It was just unexpected. Okay?"

"It's not okay," I said.

He took a cigarette from a pack that he replaced in his coat pocket. He cupped his hands and tried to light it, but the wind was blowing too hard. I took the cigarette from him and managed to light it for him, and then asked for a cigarette for myself.

"Alma," he said, handing me the pack, "let's not fight about this anymore, *please.*"

I puffed at my cigarette as we scanned each other. "You don't approve of abortion, do you?"

"I'm not sure what I think . . . it's hard to explain."

"What's hard to explain?"

"You and me, Alma . . . we're different."

"Sure, I'm pregnant . . . you're not."

"No, not that."

"What then?"

"You always seem to know what you're doing. You tell me out of nowhere that you're pregnant—and want an abortion, I might add—and you expect me . . . well, I don't know what you expect. Tell me, do you really know what you're doing?"

"No," I said. "All I know is what will happen to me if I don't get an abortion. Do you realize what Rats will do to me?" I laid a trembling hand on his arm. "I need your help, Percy. I have no one else to ask. You will help me, won't you? You won't desert me?"

We stood in silence a few moments.

"Can I ask a question?" he said.

"Yes."

"Are you absolutely sure you can't leave Rats? You can't have the baby with me?"

"I don't see how I can, Percy."

"What if you can't get an abortion? What if you can't find a doctor who would do it for you?"

"What would I do? God knows. Kill myself . . . I don't really know."

He kissed my forehead. "For the life of me I can't see how it's going to work . . . but don't worry, I won't desert you. You can count on me."

9

After he became my assistant, the little dollop of whipped cream started showing muscle.

He went to London the following week—his idea—rushing from chemist to chemist, a feverish urgency attending his every move. There was no deliberation, no interval between thought and action. He simply asked each chemist if he knew an abortionist. He'd speak in code, the kind of language you'd use with children when trying to turn an onerous task into a game. He'd say something like, "Excuse me, sir, but I have a freighter that needs unloading. Would you happen to know anyone who . . ." And the right chemist, he assumed—and he was correct—would understand what he was looking for and say, "So you're looking to unload a freighter, are you? Well, maybe I can find someone who can assist. If I do, I'll have him get in touch with you."

Someone did get in touch with Percy and told him he'd meet us in Regent's Park Zoo, at the elephant-house entrance, on Thursday afternoon, at three. We were to carry copies of *The Times,* which I thought rather odd, since quite a lot of people carry *The Times.* Ah, it would be easy enough to obtain copies of *The Times* and display them at the elephant house—but the rest of it . . . ! I had to bring two hundred pounds cash with me, much more than I had on hand. Percy took me to a queer little shop on High Street in Blackheath that had a metal grill over the window in which was displayed the most bizarre collection of accordions, golf clubs, cuff links, fur pieces, and long swords and daggers. My stomach revolted at the thought of my diamond earrings joining that sleazy jumble, and for a moment, I wondered whether we should back out. Percy had told a man we'd meet him at the zoo, true enough, and yet a conversation I had no part in was easily dismissed. So easily, in fact, that there was some doubt that the man Percy spoke to would actually appear. For another thing, Percy was not holding up well. He was becoming testy. I had no idea why he suddenly reversed himself from disapproval to passionate support of the abortion, but it was certainly a mixed blessing. He had taken to talking to me in a brisk, authoritative way, and was quick to take offense if I didn't welcome his suggestions. One did not do this sort of thing with someone who appeared always on the verge of a temper tantrum. I asked him one evening, fearing his anger, but fearing a scandal more (I have a son), whether he had given the abortionist my name, if he had given the abortionist any information that could be used to identify me. I felt I had to ask. He was outraged. He began pulling at his hair. "How could you think this of me? You must think I am an idiot. I don't know why I try to help you when it's obvious you have absolutely no respect for my judgment." Perhaps his temper was a signal that we should forget about it, after all.

Yet when that Thursday came, he took my arm, told me to relax, and assured me everything would be all right. He seemed altogether incandescent with warmth, with understanding. We were about an hour early, so we walked over to the Smithfield Market and wandered around the cluttered aisles, as little charges of anxiety went off in my belly, till two-thirty. Then we purchased copies of *The Times*, and entered the Regent's Park Zoo, which was looking rather beautiful, much more colorful than one would have imagined so late in October. The red maples had no leaves but the yellow ones were in full glory, and the beeches seemed to radiate scarlet and gold. The lawns were green, the sun shone, the peacocks and pink flamingos were suitably extravagant. Oh, it was beautiful, but not for me. I was preoccupied, frantically trying not to feel, trying to get to some numb mindless place, hardly aware even of the young man who walked beside me.

We made our way over pedestrian-only Charlbert Bridge, then through a pine grove, past a long pond where several varieties of geese live, past a truck delivering hay to some antelope, past giraffes, ostriches, and great apes. The animals were interesting, I thought, but in a hopeless sort of way. So many in these horrid little cells, so many sick with boredom, so much misery. Normally I would appreciate, for instance, the chimpanzees. But I hated the way these two chimpanzees were rocking back and forth, doing nothing but squatting in place and rocking back and forth picking at themselves with sleepy bored expressions on their faces. It was incredibly sad.

Percy paused in front of a Siberian tiger's cage, his attention snagged by the massive creature rubbing itself against the bars. He made some point about zoos, something about how they remind us of our real place in the universe—how the perfection of nature proves that people are not the ultimate power, we do not dominate the cosmos, or something to that effect—and then, like a dance partner, he placed his hand lightly in the small of my back and directed me to the elephant-house entrance, where there were several stone benches. Inside the cage itself were four or five of the saddest-looking elephants I had ever seen. We sat down and watched. The animals were huge, their smell intense. A group of schoolboys were trying to get their attention, shouting and throwing peanuts at them. Seeing the little boys, I suddenly missed Felix and felt a pang of guilt for not bringing him along, even though he adored playing with Irene who spoiled him rotten. Some mothers, I know, take their children to the zoo quite frequently, and I wondered why I was not that kind of mother, why it had never occurred to me to take Felix to the zoo, and for a moment I closed my eyes and imagined Felix sitting beside me on the bench, telling me all about the animals he'd seen at the zoo. I breathed in his little-boy smell of perspiration and sour milk. I felt his skin, the gentle weight of his hand on mine. And the next moment, I was spiraling downward, all my misgivings about abortion coming back to me: the pain, the shabbiness, the sordid meetings and arrangements, the stories of wire coat hangers and kitchen tables, the rubber fingers probing inside my body, the feeling that I had ceased being a person and had become instead a problem in need of a solution, an object apart from everything human and safe. I squeezed my eyes shut and asked God to help me. But this only depressed me more. God doesn't help women obtain abortions, I said to myself. He's probably unhappy with me for deciding to have an abortion. He probably wants to punish me.

"Are you all right, Alma?" asked my lover, patting my leg tenderly.

"I'm fine, thanks," I said, smiling falsely, feeling as sinful as a murderer, my heart hammering so loudly that I actually imagined Percy must have heard it. How crazy can you get? I tried to calm myself down by telling myself that I was not, in fact, a murderer, that the ordeal would soon be over, and that I was now at the point of meeting the physician who would abort my pregnancy. And just then, as if to make the latter thought tangible, a short, thickish man in a black trench coat appeared from the rear of the elephant house, stood for a second quite still, looking at us, his head high, as I laid a hand on Percy's arm to alert him. It lasted no more than two seconds, the squat man's glance, and then he walked toward us very quickly with little mincing strides, rising to his toes with each step. He stopped beside us and asked if he could sit on our bench.

"Yes, of course," we said.

He sat on the edge of the bench, glanced at the newspapers displayed on our laps, and then lifted his eyes to smile. It was then I noticed that his eyes were watery and red. He did have a rather kind face, I thought, with friendly wrinkles round the eyes, but he also had what looked like a nasty case of conjunctivitis. I had come prepared for a sinister-looking man, possibly a brutal one, but not a sick one. The discharge from the corners of his eyes was so abundant that the gel-like fluid had overflowed the ridges of the eyes themselves—a beastly sight. He was almost certainly contagious. Was this man the abortionist? And if he was, what did his conjunctivitis mean, I wondered, as far as the likelihood of sepsis from the surgery?

"I beg your pardon," he said, looking at me, "but I am trying to locate a young man and a woman looking for help in obtaining a certain medical service. Am I correct in assuming that you are those people?"

I was wearing a tailored navy blue suit, navy gloves, a metallic-gray blouse, and a little navy hat with a spotted half-veil that came down over my eyes and part of my nose. Woman-of-the-world was the plan, chic and well-bred. But the blouse was a little tight and I didn't like the fabric, and I was kicking myself for not wearing something else. I wished I'd worn my tweed coat, something less conspicuous and uncomfortable. A grotesquely handsome young man in a torn sweater, his head tilted at an odd birdlike angle, seemed to be staring at me.

I tried a smile. It did not feel convincing.

"Yes, you are most certainly correct," I said, nodding, trying to hold my smile steady, speaking in a voice that I imagined sounded nervous and self-conscious, thinner and higher than my usual voice.

Percy put out his hand and said, "Pleased to meet you, sir."

I leaned away from the man, staring at a little girl who was drinking water from a concrete fountain, leaning all her weight against a metal button embedded in the cement, praying that the gentleman with conjunctivitis would not offer me his hand. Without doubt, he was one of the most infectious humans I had ever seen. His eyelids had the crumbly, granulated look a sponge gets when it's run along the surface of an old bread box, and the sight of them made me wonder how many other diseases he was suffering from, besides conjunctivitis. How could I possibly allow this infectious man to touch me? On the other hand, I thought this could very well be my last chance for an abortion. An abortionist with conjunctivitis was preferable to no abortionist, was it not?

The man didn't say anything for several moments. He was looking all around the park with a great frown, darting his eyes to one thing and then another, perhaps to make sure we hadn't brought the police with us. When he seemed satisfied that we hadn't, the frown vanished from his face and a gentle smile took its place. For a couple of minutes he made stiff small talk about the park and the animals, how autumn was the most beautiful season, and how the day would be perfect if only the sun would come out. I pretended to be interested, smiling and nodding. Then he glanced at his watch and asked if he could speak bluntly.

"Please," I said.

"Are you quite sure you want to go ahead with this?"

I told him I was quite sure but would appreciate it if he would answer a few questions. Then, clasping my hands on my knees as though trying to frame my thoughts, I went through my list more briskly than I intended, my voice shaking as I spoke.

"Do a great many women use your service?"

"Quite a few."

"And are they generally satisfied?"

"Most are quite satisfied."

"How long does the procedure take?"

"About twenty minutes."

"Only twenty minutes?"

"I've never really looked at a clock but, yes, I'd say twenty minutes sounds right."

"Is it very painful?"

"Only slightly, I'd say."

And finally there was the crucial question: "And would you happen to be the gentleman who is going to perform the uh—"

"Oh, no," the man smiled, a nice little smile that stayed mostly on his eyes. His manner was kindly, not at all threatening. "No, madam, I'm the driver."

Thank you, Lord.

He explained that we were to meet him at a certain garage, and gave us the address. The garage had a broken door and his van would be parked inside. It was a red bakery van. The rear doors would be open and I was to get right in. No looking around, no hesitation. I was supposed to just hop right into the van—PDQ. Then he would drive me to the clinic. Percy, he said, should remain in our car, parked on the street adjacent to the garage. He was not to get out of our car.

I wanted to ask, Why a van? Why in the world would we be driving to the clinic in a bakery van? But Percy interrupted my train of thought and took control of the conversation. He did not at all like the idea that he was required to wait in the car while I was at the clinic. He shook his head back and forth not exactly incensed but profoundly unhappy. I imagined he was beginning to believe he might not see me again.

"I'd like to come with you," he said to the driver. "In fact, I insist on it."

The driver hesitated, as if debating how to respond; he cleared his throat and adjusted his cuffs. "I'm sorry if we neglected to clarify over the telephone," he said in a respectful voice, pursing his lips and frowning slightly, "but we only take the woman to the clinic. It's one of our rules."

"I must say, I don't think it's a very good rule," Percy said.

"A great many people are unhappy with it," the driver said, "and I really can't blame them, but you can understand that we don't want more people coming to the clinic than absolutely necessary, because . . ."—he cleared his throat again and smiled—"because we are in a precarious position, after all. We're asking you to be patient. It *is* a bother. You're quite right about that. But a small one, I think. And it's for a good reason. I don't think you should have to wait terribly long, either. No longer than an hour, I'd say."

He sounded very professional, very reasonable.

"Right," Percy said, taking a conciliatory tone, "you have to be cautious—"

"Exactly."

"But I'm sure you understand that we have to be cautious too. A convalescent should hardly be expected to submit to being hauled around London without a friend close by to look out for her."

The man blew out his cheeks. "With all due respect, sir, I do have my instructions. That's the way it has to be."

Percy didn't think so, and I felt this little tugging, tugging at my sleeve. "Would you excuse us a moment," he said, smiling at the driver, "the lady and I need to talk." Percy took my hand, and led me to the side of the elephant cage, out of earshot of the driver. He was disturbed but still under control. No desperation came from him yet. "Alma, I don't like the idea of you going off without me. And anyway, heavens alive, girl, you don't know a thing about these people. Suppose, just suppose, something went wrong. I don't mean to alarm you but"—his voice dipped to a whisper—"women have been known to die."

Almost from the moment I decided to abort my pregnancy, I'd been desperately afraid I might wind up dead from it. At the same time, I was so desperately afraid of the repercussions if word of my condition got out, that the two fears managed somehow to balance each other out. All I had to do was imagine my bloated belly, bloated like the belly of a boa constrictor after swallowing an entire lamb—huge, exceptional, monstrous—and any lingering fear of death would disappear. My only fear at the moment was that if this impasse continued any longer, I'd forever lose my chance at getting an abortion, that the whole thing would be for nothing. Abortionists, I was sure, had little use for difficult clients. I knew Percy was looking out for my welfare, but I did think he was coming on much too strong. I smiled at the driver, who just sat there watching us, a resigned, waiting expression on his face, as though he were in a long queue, and then turned back to Percy: "What in God's name are you trying to do, Percy? Now will you stop it?" I appreciated his concern, I told him, but said I'd made my decision. The driver seemed quite decent, I said. Unduly cautious perhaps, and yet surely he had ample reason to be careful. If he had been in the least unreasonable, I would walk away, I said, but as it was, the request to have Percy wait in the car seemed modest enough. It would be foolish to have come this far and turn back now.

A sudden autumn wind blew my hair into my face, my skirt tight against my legs, as I returned to the driver who again looked at his watch, said it was getting late, and then asked if I'd brought the two hundred pounds. I showed him the envelop in my purse. He gave us instructions on how to get to the garage and said he'd meet me there in an hour. He left, and Percy and I made our way quickly across the park, aiming for the exit at Fitzjohn's Avenue, where our car was parked.

The journey to the garage was a classic horror story such as only Rats, if he knew what I was doing, would have had the heart to write for me. The sky had darkened and a spray of rain fell from it like a veil. It had become chilly, uncomfortable, and Percy's mood had darkened too, a dark aura circling his head, like the halo of a saint, only in negative, a halo of darkness rather than light. The contrast between the supportive companion who entered the park with me and this miserable, anxious, irritated young man seemed to me suddenly grotesque. I honestly wished I had left him at home and taken the train into London instead. All the way to the garage, as I stared out the window at strange warehouses and factories and empty lots, he leaned forward over the steering wheel, squinting through the windshield, and whined: Hadn't I seen the driver's eyes? His eyes were living proof of the doctor's incompetence. They were an omen. How could a competent physician use such a stinker as a driver? Wasn't this a sign that he was the kind of physician who'd use a dirty knife on me and give me blood poisoning? How could I be so blind, so complacent? What was wrong with me, anyway?

By the time we reached the district that was neither Belgravia nor Covent Garden nor Chiswick, an ugly derelict area lined with sooty row houses and boarded-up factories plastered with billboards, nowhere near any place I had been before, he was properly worked up, almost crazed, occasionally punching the steering wheel with his fist, and I was feeling exhausted, as if the last remnant of life energy had been drained out of me. I had felt confident before I had gotten into the car, confident enough. But I didn't feel confident any longer. Everything about the abortion had been called into question. Even in my best moments the decision was a tenuous one to me, a thin gossamer skin held in place by desperation. I needed a lot of support to keep it together. I needed Percy's energy and certainty, the determination flowing from him, because on my own there was nothing but fear.

We parked on Boylan Terrace. It must have been the saddest street in the world, long and narrow and potholed, with rows of two- and three-story brick houses facing each other, most from the early nineteenth century, some more recent, but all decaying, forlorn, in ruins, like a nightmare, the cover on a book of dark fiction. Horror pulp. The street was empty except for a few huddled shadowy figures in doorways and a tattered old man lying unconscious in the middle of the sidewalk, his face against the concrete not ten yards from the garage with the broken door: a small barn-like structure with peeling paint and rotten boards connected to one of the houses, number 48 Boylan Terrace, which, so far as I could tell, was unoccupied.

Before I got out of the car, I turned around to look at Percy. He was looking away, his fist in his mouth, like he was afraid to say something. I waited. He took his hand out of his mouth. Then with his eyes brimming with tears, he gazed at me fixedly, as though for the last time.

"I can't let you do this," he said in a quavering voice. "If, as you made clear to me, I am responsible for the present mess, if indeed I forced myself on you, then I cannot sit by quietly and allow you to risk your life. If I did, and something was to happen to you, I'd never forgive myself. Don't do this."

I touched a fingertip to his eyelashes.

"Don't," he said again, his voice pitiful as a child's. "Please, please, please, don't get out of the car. Come home with me."

I took a pink tissue out of my purse, dabbed at his eyes, and said something to reassure him, something about the need to shut our mind to the difficulties, the need to be brave, and then opened the door. There was nothing else to do. Whether I was afraid or not, whether I might die or not, made no difference now. And I willed myself out of the car—willed myself to walk through the steady but silent rain, my shoulders straight, chin up. I tried to affect an airy, casual style. I tried to block out the thought of the old man sprawled in the middle of the sidewalk and the thought of how anomalous, how odd I must look on that London street that evening. I tried to keep my mind fixed upon the red bakery van, and upon the next step and the next and the next—until I came within a couple of yards of the garage entrance.

Then I stopped. There was something about the van and its open double rear doors. I had the sensation of someone who, sauntering along a familiar path in the dark, stumbles into a ditch. Why was the sight of the van so jarring? I took a few steps closer and had the answer: there were no windows in the rear and, if my eyes were to be trusted, no proper seat to sit on. My God, it has come to this, I thought. They intended to transport me in the dark, on the floor, as though I were a piece of freight. I was so shocked, so shaken, I couldn't move. And the odd thing was, nobody seemed to think it significant. Nobody thought it mattered. As if the laws of human decency no longer applied to me. How could the physician assume I would accept that? Did he think I'd sunk that low? That I deserved such treatment?

Once I had been determined, quite dauntless. I had been prepared for battle. All that had gone. Now, apparently beguiled by the prospect of boarding the van, yet not capable of simply walking away, I stood frozen on the strip of concrete that was the garage entrance, literally wringing my hands.

The driver came out from behind the wheel of the van. He was standing next to me, so close I could smell the gin on his breath.

"What are you waiting for?" he said.

"But there are no windows back there."

A man wearing a long, dirty overcoat walked past on the street; he was pushing an empty wheelbarrow and pulling a mongrel dog. He turned his face to me and I tried not to recoil.

The driver looked as if he had no idea and didn't care to have any idea what I was talking about. "I'm sorry, madam," he said with a frown, "but we're going to have to get going."

When I asked him if I could sit up front with him, he gave a little smile, shook his head as if humoring a child and told me, "Rules are rules, I'm afraid," and put his hands gently on my shoulders and tried to usher me into the rear of the van. I felt my shoulders contract. I wanted to push him away. I was furious but not quite furious enough because my knees felt weak with shame and fear, as if I were going to faint. Then, as I stood there, forcing myself to take deep breaths and to remain on my feet through a sheer act of will, out of the corner of my eye I recognized a figure heading toward me, walking through the fine thin drizzle, the sidewalk rippling, tremulous as a reflection on a pond. He was still far away, but he seemed familiar, and seemed to be whistling a little.

Please God, I thought, *let him take me away. I will do anything you ask of me, God, but please let him take me from here.*

I went limp and closed my eyes and waited, surprised when I opened them to see it really was him, and surprised too to feel the hairs tingling on the back of my neck as he reached for my hand, his lips curving in a faint but bold smile. I smiled back at him and put my head on his chest, breathing fast as a result of my moment of panic, blood singing in my ears, looking not at all like a prominent architect's wife, feeling a glow of relief spread through my entire body.

"I have to get away from here," I whispered.

I must have sounded very compelling to Percy for he did not ask me any questions, or indeed say anything to me. He only spoke to the driver, something polite yet definitive, then linked his arm through mine, and shepherded me slowly toward our car, through the rain that was now almost a mist. He was all savior now—a savior with a limpid maiden on his arm, hastening her out of the garage, and into the Boylan Terrace Street of nineteenth-century crumbling row houses, cobblestones and potholes. A savior, calm and assured, he paused for a well-measured moment as he opened the front door of our Daimler to give me a look straight out of his gray-blue eyes, and then, boldly, clearly, told me to sit up front next to him. If he had asked me to sit next to him at any other time, I would have refused but now I kissed his cheek and nestled my head against his shoulder.

So glad was I not to be riding in the bakery van that for a moment I had an impulse to laugh. Then I became conscious that my dress was damp, my shoes were wet, and that the cold was getting right to my bones, which reminded me that my breasts would soon become sponge-like, saturated with milk. I had somehow made up my mind that after today, my breasts would return to normal. I believed that everything would return to normal. That was not to be. I was back where I started, with breasts the size of melons, still carrying the time bomb inside my belly.

"Are you all right?" he asked.

"Yes," I said, miserably, but also feeling rather embarrassed, self-conscious, as if I'd just emerged from a hypnotic trance.

"You're alive," he said. "That's the main thing. That's all that really matters."

"I'm still pregnant. That matters too, don't you think?" My hands went to my breast. It felt to my fingers like a balloon. "Would somebody please tell me what the hell we are going to do now?"

"We could have a couple of quick ones before we got home," he said. "That's something we could do. To cheer us up."

I smiled. "A positively brilliant idea," I said, surprised to feel my mood lift, all the tearing emotion of the last few hours seeming to lift from my shoulders like a somber, heavy cloak. I wanted to drink very badly but I was also starving. Almost twelve hours since I'd eaten anything.

We found a noisy little Irish pub on Tysoe Street, a plain rectangular room with sawdust on the floors, and we both ordered steaks, which were overcooked, but I enjoyed mine anyway. We drank Scotch with beer chasers, and Percy was childishly delighted to see my spirits return, and to see the relish with which I ate my steak and chips. We didn't talk much during the meal or the drive home, but it was amazingly pleasant, considering how awful the afternoon had been. I was happy because there wasn't any need to talk or cry or bare my soul to him. What I felt was an enormous sense of relief. Suddenly, it no longer seemed important to me that I was still pregnant. I felt, oddly, illuminated by the glow of some great insight, although I had no idea what that insight was. I could not, somehow, organize my thoughts into an assessment of what had just happened or into a new vision of the future. As I sat beside Percy, my hand on his leg, I could only identify a feeling of gladness. I felt like a returning hero, a woman who had passed a difficult test without a nick, with barely a wince. I'd survived.

As for Percy, whom I loved all the more for being there for me, and more than that, for having shown how much I mattered to him, I felt I had a friend who would do anything for me. After this day, I knew what his love was about. We may have been wrong for each other in every respect; we may not have made any sense, but I would not think about it, or, indeed, about anything at all. That night, I only knew that he was meant for me; we belonged together.

10

Almost as soon as I got home, I threw myself on the bed, and fell into a deep asleep. As a rule, I don't pay much attention to my dreams and have difficulty remembering them, but that night I had one that was unusual. I was sitting at the dining-room table eating croissants and escargots with Rats and Compton Pakenham, my second husband, when I said casually, "I think I'll have my baby after we finish eating." Then I turned to the two men: "Would one of you mind helping with the delivery?" The dreams I have of my second husband and Rats are almost always unpleasant, and in this one, Pakenham was more or less true to form. He dismissed my request with a sardonic laugh, but Rats seemed unthreatening, agreeable. "Help?" he stammered. "I don't know, if you really. . . ." He was reluctant to assist in the delivery—mostly out of shyness and embarrassment—but he did assist, and quite effectively and compassionately, or so it seemed to me in the dream, and with the split consciousness that sometimes characterizes dreams, I remarked to my sleeping self that he was really sweet and that a woman could do much worse than to have such a helpful, gentle man as her husband, a kind of latter-day saint.

That's all that I remember of the dream, that and the fact that as soon as I woke up I felt an inner peace I hadn't felt in weeks: the inner peace of someone who has been clinging to a ledge and at last lets go. There was an easy, perfectly simple solution. It was to go ahead and have the baby. After feeling inundated with fear, when for so long it seemed that suicide was preferable to having the baby, deciding at last to go through with the birth felt like a sort of liberation. The answer wasn't to obtain an abortion—and I even smiled at myself for having once believed it was—the answer was to embrace the baby, love the baby, make it mine. I was convinced that if Rats discovered I was pregnant with Percy's baby he'd divorce me, that I'd lose Felix and my home, lose everything that was dear to me, but if I could convince Rats that the baby was his and just went ahead and had it, I wouldn't have to lose anything. My life would go on as before.

All I had to do was sleep with Rats again.

What I did not yet realize, not until I was preparing a pot of tea a couple of hours later, was that I also had to tell Percy. The implications of that affected me like a sudden rise in blood pressure, and I turned quickly to sit down at the kitchen table. I would have preferred not telling him but he had to know I intended to convince Rats that the baby was his, and that the baby's true paternity would have to remain our secret; otherwise the whole plan would be ruined. I could keep it from him for a few months, sure, but not much longer and certainly not after I told Rats I was pregnant and, of course, even if I could find a way to keep it from him, it wouldn't be fair. He might've been only a boy, but he was still the baby's father. I'd have to tell him. I'd had enough dissembling. Somehow I felt that any more dissembling would strangle me. I'd have to tell him and pray to God he'd understand.

But how, tell him what? What do you say to a proud boy like Percy? Do you just go up to him and say, "Look, darling. I hope this doesn't upset you, but I've decided it would be better for everyone if you gave up your rights to the baby and let Rats assume . . ."

What would he do? Would he become resentful, jealous?

Would he cry? Was there a chance he'd refuse to cooperate? Was there a chance he might even threaten to tell Rats? For perhaps two hours—that is, until about eleven-thirty—this sequence of questions repeated itself over and over in my imagination, until I decided finally that I simply could not imagine what he'd do; I couldn't picture telling him at all. And then the thought occurred to me that I might not have to if I could convince him to quit and go to school in London, as he said he wanted. I could send him money. He would be out of the way, and I could go on with my life and have the baby.

But I did not embrace so obvious a solution. The fact is I didn't want him to go away; more exactly, it wasn't in me to send him away. I tried to force myself to imagine him living in London, but all I could see was him in a flat all by himself, lonely, forlorn, inconsolable without me. For a moment I even pictured him doing to himself what his mother had done to herself. The mere thought brought me to my feet and convinced me that my task was to protect him from that tragic end and keep him with me the rest of my life, or his, if I had to.

There was no getting around it: I would have to tell him that I planned to sleep with Rats.

The irony of the situation was not lost on me. You sometimes hear about a married woman in the midst of an affair confessing to her husband that she is sleeping, or intends to sleep, with another man. Here I was about to confess to my lover that I intended to sleep with my husband, desperately worried that he'd disapprove, and felt a chill of amusement but also—mainly—anxiety.

Then the thought crossed my mind that Percy and I could have this conversation at the Cotswolds. I became slightly cheered by the idea of trying to recapture something of the spirit that had visited us yesterday in the restaurant and by the thought that it would do us good to have a holiday. Except for the trips to the pawnshop in Blackheath and to London for the abortion, we hadn't gone anywhere in weeks. Hadn't he said he wanted to picnic with me at the Cotswolds?

The fact that I still had no idea how to explain it to him, that I couldn't even imagine myself explaining it to him, did not seem to matter any longer. I would deal with everything later, at the picnic. So the following morning, after having wangled the use of the car for the entire day, Percy and I started off with a basket full of provisions and a bottle of wine. It was a fine morning for a drive, sun struggling through mist, neither too warm nor too cold, the air not even close to chilling; the ice that had recently formed at the sides of the road was now melted, and for the moment any misgivings I had about my mission were forgotten.

He hummed as he drove, loosened his collar and tie, and I kept glancing at him, receiving enormous reassurance from the sight of him sitting there so serenely, humming softly to himself. From time to time I joined in, and at one point he asked me to sing something for him—Gilbert and Sullivan. I agreed and sang "Tit Willow" as loudly and woefully as I could. I was not in good voice. As a matter of fact, I was in exceptionally bad voice that morning but he didn't seem to notice or care. He was actually laughing. When he asked me to sing, "Here's A Pretty How-De-Do!" it occurred to me that in a few moments I would be handing him a pretty how-de-do of my own, but managed to brush that thought aside. I'll sing whatever he wants, I thought; he's the one whom this outing is for.

He wanted to visit the tomb at Belas Knap, which was on a hill above Humblebee Wood, two miles south of Winchcombe. The entrance passages to the various burial chambers had been sealed for eons, but had been restored and were now open to the public. Percy was very excited about visiting them; the ceilings were vaulted and damp, soggy with the moisture of centuries, and he thought they might be home to bats, possibly evil spirits.

Inside, there was the smell of mould and decaying leaves, and where the ground tiles were damp, the footing was difficult. I slipped at each step. No one was down there except for two old women and a small child. They were pottering along preoccupied, minding their business. So when I stopped to examine a prehistoric wall and was bemused, for the moment, by the sheer age of the hieroglyphics, he wasn't deterred by the risk of making a public spectacle, and leaned over and kissed me on the mouth with almost passionate intensity. After kissing for some length, we moved on, up the stairs, out into the daylight, and I looked at his face and was surprised at how sad he appeared.

His mother was on his mind. During lunch, while we sat on top of a pretty hill which looked down to wheat-colored fields, drinking our wine and eating our curried chicken, our plates balanced on our laps, he explained how his mother, a woman from a middle-class family who was well-educated and comfortably off, had met his father, a plumber. His father was attempting to open a clogged drain at his mother's parents' house but then became distracted by a ray of sunlight. First the ray of sunlight shone on his tools, then on the drain, then on his hands, and finally, his eyes. After a moment, he looked up and smiled. He smiled because he saw the woman who was to become Percy's mother holding a pocket mirror; she had been reflecting rays of sunlight into his eyes.

"She seduced him?" I asked.

"Seems that way."

He showed me a photograph of her. "Isn't she beautiful?"

I said "very" though she wasn't at all beautiful. In the photo she was thin just like Percy, but her skin had no color, and she wore no makeup. She was posing so stiffly, she looked pathetic.

"She always photographs well," he said.

"I thought you said she killed herself?"

"She did."

I waited a moment for him to fill in the gap.

"The effort it took to get along with my father was too much for her. I used to hear the two of them fighting, my father calling her stupid." His tone was objective, matter of fact; this told me that something was wrong, that I really shouldn't have asked him about her death.

"Are you all right?" I asked.

He looked at me, tried to say something, and shook his head, looking suddenly no more than thirteen or fourteen years old. Words did not come to his lips until I put my arms around him and rocked him, and then he said, "I love you, Alma. I can't tell you how much." This was not a happy position for me to be in: to be comforting him for the loss of his mother one minute and then the next to have to tell him that he was going to have to relinquish paternity rights over his child. How was I to break it to him? What made me think that coming here would make it any easier?

The sky was darkening, a front moving in, and it was getting colder, the afternoon settling into a sort of predusk chill, almost uncomfortably raw. Gulls cried overhead, and far below, a triangle of three full-sized deer followed by two brown speckled fawns raced across the wheat towards the line of trees at the edge of the field, galloping as if they had just spotted a group of hunters.

I looked at my watch and saw that it was after three. Get on with it, I coached myself, otherwise it'll never happen. And so, after we'd cleaned up and moved to a flat slab of rock on the edge of the bluff, looking out over the fields of wheat shining in the dying sunlight, his face sometimes nuzzling my hair, both of us seeming quite relaxed, I said, "There's something I need to talk over with you. Rats is going to know I'm pregnant in a very short while."

I had an impulse simply to wait in silence as Percy figured out for himself what I was going to say. More than anything else, I wanted to avoid this entire conversation, to stretch out and close my eyes and drift far away, through the sky, into the clouds, and leave behind all thought of Rats and Percy and my pregnancy, but then I just blurted, "I have to make the pregnancy acceptable to him. It won't be pleasant but I see no other way out of this."

Percy said nothing, and I had the strange feeling that I had spoken much more clearly than I actually had, that my statement left no room for ambiguity. Which probably explains why I thought he wasn't serious when he said, "What won't be pleasant?"

I searched his face for some hint of irony. Surely he must have understood that I intended to sleep with Rats. How could he not? Yet I saw no irony. None.

"What?" I asked, momentarily confused.

"How will you make the pregnancy acceptable to him?"

"By persuading him he's the father."

A few more awkward moments passed as I watched him pulling scraps of the meager grass that bordered the stone we were sitting on. Then he said, frowning, "And how will you do that?"

"Stop it, Percy."

"Stop what? I'd like to know how you plan to persuade him he's the baby's father."

"Jesus Christ."

He continued to frown at me, his eyes screwed up as though he couldn't properly see, and then in a plaintive voice that combined irritation and despair, said, "So you're saying that you and Rats are going to be sleeping with each other again?"

"The last thing in the world I want is to sleep with him again.

I'd sooner cut off my right arm. It's just that it has to be done; otherwise I'd lose Felix."

"How many times?" he asked.

I waited; I didn't understand.

"How many times do you intend to sleep with him?"

"Just once."

"And then he'll think he's the father?"

"Oh please, Percy, don't get upset—"

"He'll think—he'll think. . . . God," he said. "I don't believe this."

"It'll just be that one time, I promise, then everything will go back to normal."

"When are you going to sleep with him?"

"In a day or two, probably."

"Where?"

"In his bed—in his study."

"What do you plan to say to him, or will you say anything to him?"

"You're making it much harder than it has to be."

"I'm not making it harder than it has to be! What do you plan to say to him?"

"*What do I plan to say to him?* I don't know—whatever I have to."

"Will you tell him you love him?"

"What kind of question is that? I don't have to answer a question like that."

"You most certainly do have to answer. I want to know. Will you tell him you love him?"

"I don't know. If I have to I suppose I will. What choice do I have? Now let's drop it."

"What if he wants to sleep with you again?"

"I told you already, I'll only sleep with him once."

"What if he insists?"

I just looked at him.

"Do you still plan on sleeping with me?"

"Oh, Percy."

"Just tell me if you intend to continue sleeping with me. I think I'm entitled to an answer, don't you?"

"Of course I intend to continue sleeping with you. Why are you being like this?"

And so we went back and forth, him asking increasingly hostile challenging questions, me attempting to provide serious answers, and then him blowing my answers off, taking no heed of the pragmatics of the situation, none whatever. There was something faintly masochistic in his manner, particularly, I thought, when he began asking me what sort of relationship he'd have with the baby, as though he found it appealing to imagine himself humiliated. If he wasn't going to be allowed to be the baby's father, he asked, what would he be to the baby? Would he be anything other than the baby's chauffeur?

And again, I tried to reassure him; I told him he'd be the child's dear dear friend, just as he is Felix's, but he again refused to listen.

"Do you honestly think Rats would make a better father than I?"

"Percy, this has nothing to do with who'd be the better father. Now stop it."

"Do you think Rats would love the baby as much as I?"

"This is absurd."

"I want an answer."

"You'd be a far superior father."

"You're lying a little, aren't you? You think I'm too young to be a father, don't you? You think a child would be ashamed to have a chauffeur for a father?"

"This conversation is not going anywhere."

"Where did you expect it to go?"

"Not in an endless circle of resentment, I'll tell you that."

"You thought I'd be glad that you're sleeping with Rats once again and that I'm losing my baby?"

"No, of course not, but I was hoping for your . . ." I searched for the right word. "Support," I finally said.

"My support!" he said, his voice rising.

"Can't you try to be an adult about this," I cried. "This is not something I want. I hate the idea, Percy! Everything in me recoils at the idea. But it's something I have to do. We have to accept it." I looked into his eyes to see if he understood. "We were having sex and I got pregnant. Yes, it's a piece of incredibly bad luck but it happens sometimes. We played Russian roulette and we lost. Now I have to pay the price by sleeping with a man who disgusts me, and you have to give up paternity. That's a tragic thing, I suppose. Life is often tragic."

"How righteous you are."

I had an impulse to tell him how immature he sounded, but checked myself and answered gently, "Should I be ashamed? Would that make you happy? I'm doing this only because I must. When I decided to tell Rats that I couldn't sleep with him any longer, that I wanted a bedroom of my own, I was determined to never have sex with him again. Do you have any idea what it's like to have sex with him—to be disgusted right down to the bottom of your guts? Do you have any idea what it's like to go to bed knowing you might be awakened at any moment by someone who regards you as a piece of merchandise, his private piece of meat? Do you have any idea?" Then I remembered something quite specific, something especially vivid and ugly about my sexual relationship with Rats that now I realize I should have kept to myself. Surely I must have known it was the wrong thing to say—to share. How could I not have? Yet I said it anyway, hoping to win his sympathy. "Do you know what his face looks like when he reaches his climax? Did you know that—can you possibly imagine—that he grins, an insolent mocking grin that seems to be saying, 'Pretty good for an old man, don't you think?' the sort of grin, Percy, that makes everything decent in your life feel like a joke."

"Yet you're going to sleep with him?"

"This is one of the hardest things I've ever done in my life. I was hoping you'd understand."

"I'm sorry, I don't."

"*What* don't you understand?"

"If he's such a monster, if it's so dreadful to sleep with him, then why in God's name don't you just leave him? What I don't understand is why you don't just tell him to go to hell."

Here is where I lost my temper. I have looked back at this moment a hundred times and sought desperately to understand why I couldn't accept his failure to be supportive. Wasn't I aware of how difficult this was for him, how young and inexperienced he was, and how proud? Why couldn't I have taken him in my arms and given him the time he needed to digest. I should have been patient; I should have allowed him his show of pride. But I didn't allow him any.

Instead, I cried, "Felix! I can't leave because of Felix. I'd lose him. Do I have to spell it out for you? What the hell is wrong with you, Percy?" I leapt to my feet, turned my back on him, my whole body tensed, and uttered a piercing shriek like a cat whose paw has been trod on—all so unexpected that Percy was startled.

"All right, all right," he said, now on his feet too, his set lips and pinched nostrils signifying revulsion. "Sleep with him if you have to. I understand. You have my blessing. That's what you want, isn't it?"

"How dare you patronize me!"

He made no answer, and we didn't talk at all the remainder of the afternoon. He drove home too fast, his mouth clamped tight, as if he had swallowed his lips. I only looked out the window and at the vertebrae at the back of his neck. It was malevolent bone. I thought: I am alone in this.

11

Why then later that night did I find Percy in my arms? Why did I let him kiss my eyelids and take my breast in his mouth? Why did I let him arouse in me the same sensations as before, as though they would always be there, waiting for him? Why did he put his ear on my belly, trying to discover the heartbeat of a baby that would be given to another man? And why did I again feel that we, of all the men and women in the world, belonged to each other?

I do not know. I tried not to think about our relationship, why I found him absurd one minute and irresistible the next, or, indeed, what lay ahead for us in the future—how could I? I left that to fate, just as I always had. Why we became lovers, and why we continued, I could not say. I still cannot. I only know that he made me happy, that the threads of his life seemed woven in with mine, and that no misunderstanding or challenge from the outside seemed capable of coming between us. Not permanently. Not altogether.

After sleeping with him, and then thinking about the situation the following morning, I became very calm. I was surprised at how calm I felt. I told myself that a boy Percy's age will always be jealous regardless of the explanation his lover gives when he discovers that she has slept, or intends to sleep, with another man. It's the only way a boy Percy's age can react. Just don't talk about it or remind him that he ever had any reason to be jealous, and he will forget. Yesterday was the first day. Every day that comes after will be easier.

I made my move on Rats two days later. It came after an evening in which the four of us—Percy, Irene, Felix and I—spent working on a jigsaw puzzle in the drawing room. We looked like a perfectly happy family sprawled out on the floral carpet in that large but over-heated Edwardian room, with its large chairs and fringed sofas and bookcases with glass fronts, the fireplace going full blaze, the pieces of the puzzle, a Rembrandt self-portrait, spread out before us. It was an extremely complicated puzzle with thousands of interlocking pieces that we had begun assembling the previous day. Rats had been involved in the puzzle initially; he usually became involved in selecting and connecting the puzzle pieces that had straight edges, but as those pieces had already been connected, he had given up and was now reading a book, tortoiselike, in his gilt-framed armchair.

From time to time Percy glanced at me with long, penetrating looks, but didn't speak. I wasn't really feeling very well, though I was trying to appear that I was. I felt heavy and depressed. My immediate preoccupation was how and when to get into bed with Rats, and whether I could get there without anybody noticing. I hated the idea of sneaking around at night. But mostly I hated the idea of getting back into bed with my husband. Instead of the long, slender body with its smooth cheeks and jutting ribs, I would be lying next to the swollen, hairy stomach of an aging, almost old man, whose upper lip peeked out like a slice of raw sausage. *And I've kissed that mouth!* Escaped prisoners must feel something like this when the searchlight beams on them from the guard tower. Having so long prayed for release from sexual servitude, having begged fate for deliverance from his bed, the thought of revisiting it felt like a form of surrender, a ritual sacrifice, the slaughtering of a lamb on the altar to appease the threatening god, and the essence of every physical encounter from every night I had ever slept with him concentrated once again horribly in my brain.

After we gave up on the puzzle and Irene took Felix to bed, I went up to my room and did some deep breathing. Breathe in. Breathe out. Deep breathing is supposed to help you relax.

Actually, it did help. The shot of whiskey helped, too.

I checked the clock. Good, nine fifteen. I'll give it five more minutes, I thought, to make sure everyone is settled and then I'll head down to Rats' study. What was the big deal, anyway? When compared to my abortion fiasco, sleeping with Rats was nothing. Disgust would not deter me; I had confidence in my decision. In the normal course of life, I told myself, there were many worse things than having intercourse with Rats. He could penetrate my flesh but not my heart or soul. And, the truth was, I did have plenty of experience opening my flesh up to him without anything really awful happening. What I had survived before, I could survive again.

I took two or three more shots of whiskey and made my way down the stairs, the back ones, clutching the banister, taking deep breaths to steady myself, my plan becoming clearer and less worrisome the closer I came to Rats' study. I decided that however much Rats and I distrusted each other—and I still did not know how much he distrusted me—I would behave as if everything between us was ordinary, open, aboveboard. Everything depended on being casual and light-hearted. I knew that if he suspected me of manipulating him, not merely might he question whether the baby was his, he might refuse to sleep with me, and I tried to take comfort from the fact that he had given no indication of losing interest in my body, and that he had never in all the years we'd been together rejected an opportunity to sleep with me. The slightest flutter of my eyes could arouse him. Indeed, during our last sexual encounter, he could barely control himself. I must, I thought, simply aim to get it over with as quickly as possible so I could return to my own bedroom before Percy appeared. And by the time I stood outside Rats' door preparing to knock, brightening my smile, I thought myself well prepared, confident.

He must have heard me.

"Come in," shouted Rats. "Come on in." The smile he gave me could be described as more than friendly, almost effusive.

"There was something I wanted to talk to you about," I said, feeling feverish and a little tipsy as I caught sight of his green crepe de chine pajamas and stepped into his study, which seemed now markedly more squalid than before. It was still his study, the same books and pictures of sailing ships and Napoleonic battles covered the walls, the same frayed but magnificent tapestry behind his drawing table, his collection of porcelain tigers and lions on the mantelpiece, a fire burning cozily beneath, but now it had clothing on the floor and leftover food on his desk. Now it also had a narrow bed in it with a headboard of dark varnished wood and a silver comforter that looked like a lot of coins sewn together. Beside his bed was a small nightstand upon which he had a glass and a decanter of sherry. The thought of him drinking and eating and sleeping there infused me with a disagreeable mixture of pity and contempt. Poor man, how far he's fallen! And how badly I've treated him, although that moment he seemed forgiving enough, willing to let bygones remain bygones. He had been reading a book in bed and sat up when I entered, pulling his comforter over the wispy white hairs on his chest with one hand, raising the other to his scalp in a vain attempt to smooth it down.

"My goodness," he said. "My goodness, my goodness. This *is* a surprise."

Before I could offer an explanation, he asked me if I was familiar with the book he was reading, a novel called *Stay of Execution*.

I said I wasn't.

"It's really very good."

"Oh?"

He said it was the story of a man who feels old and depressed, and whose thoughts turn to suicide. He insisted on reading aloud a passage in which the author, in the form of a dialogue between the main character and a girl he is trying to discourage from marrying him, gives his opinion on elderly men with young wives:

" *'Elderly men like to marry young girls, and after a bit it's hell for both.'*

" *'Why?'*

" *'Because it's naturally annoying to a young girl to see her husband mouldering while she still feels frisky. To see the bare patch on the back of his head growing bigger and shinier. To have the shock, one day, of coming across most of his teeth grinning at her out of a glass of water. And there are other things, besides.'*

" *'What things?'*

" *'Well—if you will have me enter into physiological details—a woman, let's put it, always wants more than a man. And when a man's a good deal older, she wants a good deal more than him. A good deal more than he can give her. It takes all his time for a young man to keep pace with a young girl. And an old man hasn't a chance of doing it. And then—she usually goes somewhere else to make up the deficiency.'* "

"Sounds interesting," I said, wondering why he was reading such a book and why he wanted to share it with me now. Was it to tell me that he saw himself as an elderly man married to a young woman he can't satisfy? Or was he trying to say he knew I'd gone elsewhere to make up for his deficiency? Or was he simply saying he had begun thinking about suicide?

He said, "You can read it when I'm through, if you're interested. I should be finished with it by tomorrow."

"Thank you. That's very thoughtful of you. But I'm reading

something else right now." The fact is everything about his book depressed and overwhelmed me and I wanted only to distance myself from it, forget about it. I could not be thinking about such things at this moment. "And anyway," I said, "I really didn't come here to talk about—"

"I was just thinking you'd enjoy it, that's all."

I thanked him again, seated myself on the edge of the bed beside him, and looked at him with what I hoped was an affectionate expression, trying to get myself into a seductive frame of mind, and then, a moment later, found myself saying, "I was thinking about your last visit to my bedroom and thought that you and I . . . that both of us . . . that we might want to complete what we started."

"Complete what we started?"

"Yes."

"I don't quite follow."

"I hadn't been feeling well that morning, and hoped you'd understand and give me a second chance."

He yawned, hugely, scratched his underarm. "What morning are you referring to? *What* are you referring to?"

I began playing with the hairs on Rats' neck. "Three weeks ago . . . when we tried to make love but I couldn't quite hold up my end. Surely you remember."

"Yes," he said without a smile. "I remember."

I looked away, overcome by a sense of unreality, astonished by my explicitness, my audacity. This is going to be a very long evening, I said to myself, and then used what little strength I had left in my body to laugh and say out loud:

"Am I being too forward?"

Perplexity was all that showed on his face.

I briefly considered slipping into bed and attempting to make love wordlessly, just getting down to business, but I shrank from so direct an approach, the lack of subtlety. Still, I thought it might be wise to get started right away, to get to the point immediately. Action seemed far less problematic than silence. You will be aghast no matter what you do, I told myself. So quickly, defiantly, I turned off his reading lamp, leaving only the glow of the fireplace to illuminate the room, removed my robe, pulled off my nightgown, and slipped between the sheets.

I tried to pull him down and undo his pajama bottoms, but his body was like dead weight. This did not offend or unnerve me but I could go no further without his cooperation.

"Let's take your pajamas off, Rats."

His body could not have gone more rigid if I had poured ice water on him.

"I'm sorry," he said.

"It's all right."

"It's just—"

"What?"

"I don't know."

"Am I shocking you?"

"Shocking me?"

"I'm being too aggressive?"

"No. It's just—"

"You don't approve?"

He sat up, leaning his head back to look at me, but immediately lowering his lids. "It's not a matter of approving or disapproving, Alma. It's a matter of not understanding. I don't know quite how to put this without sounding unduly suspicious, but *something* in your behavior, and I wish to God I understood what, seems peculiar. I simply don't understand what you're trying to accomplish."

I sat up too. I smiled into his face and took hold of his hand, and spoke in a voice that seemed to me, all of a sudden, strangely hilarious. "Pleasure! Physical pleasure—that's what I'm trying to accomplish. Is that so terribly, terribly hard to understand, the idea that we might once have given each other, that we still might give each other, pleasure?"

Where did these words come from? My overstrained nerves, no doubt, and the oddity of the whole situation, the fact that our positions were reversed; he was the one who was now reticent, the one who'd rather read or go to sleep, and I was the needy one, the one desperately attempting to seduce. But whom was I desperately attempting to seduce? Not someone I found attractive. That was the hilarious part. I was desperately trying to seduce a man whose body had always inspired in me something quite close to revulsion. And I wanted, oh, how I wanted at that moment to be somewhere else—to be somewhere where I could be free to scream or smash dishes.

Nonetheless, I had my job to do. Having launched myself on this absurd track, I felt committed to it. "I'm sorry," I said. "I should have been more deliberate. Or warned you. It's just that I've been celibate for a very long time and my needs seem to have gotten the better of me. Perhaps we should start all over again. Perhaps I should put my nightgown back on and you should undress me?"

My desperation was touching. At least it ought to have been touching. Any other man would have taken pity on me—any other than Rats. He gazed at me in dismay.

"What do you say?" I said.

When he didn't answer, I said, "Yes, I know," feeling rather like a blind woman trying to demonstrate her knowledge of architecture, "I'm not following the script—the silent submissive woman script, the pure and wilting little flower script. I know I've been much too forward."

He held up his large white paw, the one I wasn't grasping, in protest.

"Or maybe I should have told you how ravishing you are. You know, you really are quite attractive. I suppose a woman should tell her husband how ravishing he is when she wants to seduce him. Please accept my apology, Rats. I honestly thought we'd been married long enough not to have to worry about a lot of silly preliminaries."

"It's all right, really, don't worry about it, please," he said, withdrawing his enormous hand and leaning back on his pillow, studying me from a distance.

I saw no friendship in his eyes. Wrinkles darkened his forehead, brows beetling. Something else had to be done immediately. What? I considered touching his private area. Would that help or confuse him even more? A deep romantic kiss on the lips? Would that reassure him or provide one more piece of evidence that I was overplaying my hand and couldn't be trusted? I had no way of knowing and so decided, finally, to try to slow things down.

"What are you thinking about?" I asked.

"Nothing, really."

"Rats, darling, do you despise me for behaving like a fool that last time, when you tried to make love to me?"

"Despise you?"

"Yes, despise me. Something tells me that you're carrying a grudge against me. I know you are."

"Alma," he said.

"Yes, Rats?"

He pushed himself up and stared at me from beneath his brows. In the indirect light, his features were vague, covered by shadow, but I could tell that he was about to say something serious and embarrassing. "Did it ever occur to you—"

He stopped.

"Did what ever occur to me?"

"The fact that you and I haven't slept together for six months—"

"Yes?"

"The fact that for six whole months you've slept in a separate bedroom. Did it ever occur to you how that made me feel?"

I remained silent.

"You never thought how it affected me?"

"You never complained, darling. I thought you had become used to it."

"For six whole months you haven't made love with me or even given me a kiss, except some absurd peck on the cheek. Not a *kiss!* No, I never became used to it. Nor would any husband—"

"Rats, darling—"

"May I finish?"

"Yes, of course—"

"I was patient. I just thought it was a phase you were going through. I was very, very patient. And then three weeks ago you told me I could make love to you, bored as you could be with the whole thing, and you treated me like a rapist! How in the world could you even look me in the eye after that? How could I look you in the eye? I'd have been astonished if we ever smiled at each other again, but now *this*—"

Well, he was correct.

Except for one thing: he neglected to mention that I treated him like a rapist because he had acted like one. But I held my tongue, even though the memory of that encounter overwhelmed me once again, together with the even greater feeling of desolation that accompanied the need to falsify myself. Which is not to say that I was angry with him. On the contrary, it seemed to take an enormous act of courage for him to bring up these painful episodes, for they were painful to him. Rats, usually so reserved and superficial, was laying his feelings bare, and I could not help but feel impressed. At the same time, there was a definite element of hostility in what he was saying, and a new notion began making its way into my consciousness: that his sexual reticence might be a long-term condition and could prove highly resistant to influence. And it occurred to me that unless I injected enormous quantities of gentleness into the proceedings, there was a good chance I might have to attempt this again, and without any guarantee of success. Above all, I realized that I had to make him feel safe with me and so, looking him straight in the eye, spoke as sincerely and sweetly as I could.

"Rats, darling . . . take a moment and explain to me what I need to do to get you to sleep with me again?"

"There's nothing *to* explain. I simply couldn't bear a repetition of the scene that happened last time we tried to make love."

"You feel bitterness against me, Rats?"

After a while he said, "Yes, I do. I can't deny it but I do."

"Oh, Rats."

"Since we're being open with each other, let me tell you that it was a nightmare to me, perhaps the worst memory of my entire life."

"Look," I said in the straightest, most sincere tone I could manage, "I know I put you through hell; I know how horrible I was to you," and I put my hands together in a gesture of prayer, and began rocking back and forth. "Would it be possible . . . do you think you could manage, for just a moment, to pretend that we're not who we are. Darling, could you perhaps pretend that we're a young married couple, just starting our lives together?"

He said nothing.

"Tell me, darling, is it too late for me? Have I exhausted my last chance?"

He remained silent but seemed to be listening.

"What if I say I'm not going to be stupid anymore or cry, or anything? What if I am really, really sorry about my behavior three weeks ago and beg you to forgive me? Will you give me another chance?"

"I'd like to, of course, but . . ."

"But what?"

He moved away to pour himself a glass of sherry and I heard the neck of the sherry decanter rattling against the rim of the glass.

"How can you expect me to believe you? You haven't done one single thing to make me believe I can trust you."

I did not say: You can believe me because your love for me ought to tell you that I'm speaking the truth. Those sorts of declarations were immaterial at the moment. His distrust was palpable. Yet even then I knew he wanted to believe me, though probably he was telling himself he shouldn't. He had clear proof from our last attempt three weeks ago that I didn't want to sleep with him, and yet I thought there was still a doubt in his head—or rather, a hope—that I might be able to convince him that he was wrong. We both knew it.

"There's nothing I can say that's going to make you trust me. I know that. All I'm asking for is a chance. One more chance."

I took his hand again and he did not withdraw it. I could tell that he was softening somewhat; no longer was he the rancorous grand inquisitor he had been only moments before. But the grim straight-jacket tightness remained in the muscles of his back and neck, and also his lips were clamped together. The reconciliation was incomplete. We both knew that too.

"You're holding something back, aren't you?" I said. "Is there something else you need to tell me?"

"Not really, Alma," he said. "I've already told you. I don't know what you're doing here. Honest to God, we both know you have no use for me."

"That's not true."

"Not true? Look at the way we've been living—the way we've been sleeping apart from each other, in separate bedrooms. You call that a marriage? I honestly don't know why you married me. It certainly wasn't because you found me attractive."

"That's not true."

"Not that I blame you—look at me, I'm old. I have a harelip."

"Please, darling," I said, "I've told you over and over, you're one of the most attractive men I've ever known."

"I know, and I know you like that I've got some money and I'm fairly well-known, but that's apparently not enough to make you want to sleep with me."

"I *do* want to sleep with you, darling. Won't you please believe me?"

He leaned back on his pillow and stared at the ceiling, his voice sinking and deepening to that tone I so much desired, as he said, "I do so wish I could believe you. I've missed sleeping with you, you know . . . more than I can say."

"Well," I said as I curled my toes on his ankle, "I'm here now."

"Very well, you're here. You're here now."

"Yes, darling."

"Will you be here tomorrow?"

This I took to be the crucial question. His willingness to sleep with me hinged on my answer, and I knew precisely what had to be said:

"Oh yes, my darling!"

And so I lied. Not with any thought of lying. Not with any thought that I was manipulating and using him, treating him as a fool. Not with any thought of the immensity of my deception, my betrayal. My guilt was already established and so couldn't be undone, wasn't even considered. What mattered to me most, the only thing in fact, was to get Rats—to be crude—to ejaculate inside me. If I failed to move rapidly, I might preclude, once and for all, the possibility of ever obtaining a legitimate father for my unborn child. All this passed through my mind with the swiftness with which a wave hits the shore, a blast of seawater bearing sand and salt and shell, and all sorts of seaweed and crabs and jellyfish. And just as, when the wave withdraws, there is a sudden silence and stillness, so my feelings for Rats, in the next moment, became all at once silent and still, and I found myself sitting there in bewilderment, staring into his dark eyes, with no thought of loathing or malice. In this dazed condition, without rehearsing the words before I spoke them, I opened my arms and said, "I'll be here tomorrow and tomorrow—"

"And tomorrow?"

"Yes, darling! And tomorrow!"

"You've said to me . . . you've said to me, 'I want to sleep with you . . .' "

"Yes, Rats!"

"But you've never said to me, 'My love, I want to be your wife again.' Alma, can you tell me, tell me do you love me and want to be my wife again?"

Another crucial question, and again there was only one possible answer: "Yes, my love, I do, I want to be your wife again."

"My darling, my beautiful Alma . . ."

"And I do so want to sleep with you now. Do you mind if I sleep with you now, darling? You know, you would be making me a very happy woman."

"Do I mind?"

"I'm throwing myself at your mercy."

He lay down beside me and looked me in the face, "More than anything I want, deep down in my deepest heart, I want to make love with you—"

"Don't say another word," I said and swooped down on top of him, my mood lifting as if by magic, and I pressed my lips to his while once again tugging at his pajama bottoms. My heart was racing, which made no sense at all, because I'd never been genuinely attracted to Rats—not even close. Yet there was no mistaking the strength of my excitement. Could it have been so strong precisely because it made no sense at all, an instance of that special, perverse kind of excitement that comes from having sexual relations with someone you know you shouldn't be having relations with, whom you have every reason to be repelled by? Of course it could just as easily have been so strong because I had been working so hard to persuade Rats of the authenticity of my desire that I'd actually succeeded in persuading myself. Then too, it might have been because the Rats who had repelled me, the Rats who made love to me as if he were racing against time, was the complete opposite of the Rats who was with me now, a Rats who was shy and hesitant and self-effacing. Or perhaps, on the other hand, this was simply my body's way of telling me that I had been carrying on my affair with my chauffeur long enough and should become a wife again. I honestly did not comprehend it myself. All I knew is that I circled Rats' body with my own, and pressed him into me as hard as I could, squeezing him till I groaned. When I let go, I was laughing. He sank onto the side of the bed as if I'd given him a drug.

"Forgive me for being so comical," he said, his white hair tumbled over his forehead and his eyes wide. "I must be out of practice."

"You were fine," I said, and I meant it.

"Just think, just think, if you hadn't wanted me so badly."

"I can't imagine," I said covering us with the sheets and comforter, "how you could think I might not want you."

He slept deeply, spooning against my side, as if we had been sleeping together every night for a decade, as if some heavy and persistent barrier had finally dissolved and my husband and I suddenly found ourselves in harmony, at peace. Nevertheless, my head was filled with urgent calculations: the time was 10:47 and I couldn't stay in bed another minute because, I knew, I needed to get back to my own bedroom before Percy came in. Percy came through my door at eleven o'clock, the same time every night. I didn't want to find out how he would react to the discovery that I'd been with Rats; I also wondered what to tell Rats now, how to get myself out of his bed without offending, worrying how he might react if he knew I had not really intended to remain with him the entire night, and had no intention of ever sleeping with him again.

But then I thought, there'd be plenty of time to smooth him out later. Now there was a need to hurry.

I tried to get out of bed without waking him but I could only manage getting one foot onto the floor.

"What is it, Alma?"

I had imagined myself to be very calm, very reasonable, and yet no calm or reasonable words came to mind. A faint tremor in my stomach warned me that my leave-taking would result in a certain awkwardness—worse than awkwardness, ugliness— since it might expose me as a manipulator, a liar. After all, I had told him I loved him, and that he could believe in me, and that I would share his bed with him from now on—that I intended to be his wife again. A graceful separation, I realized, would be impossible. It would not be graceful, and he would suffer; in fact, he would be desperate, he would be furious, he would be shattered.

I spent a moment reflecting on the answer I should give. This was the best I could contrive:

"Well, darling, the bed is very narrow, not really designed for a married couple, you know. I don't think it will do, I'm afraid I just can't get used to it. My back is already killing me. Would you mind terribly if I went back . . . if I went back to my own bedroom, just for tonight?"

"We could sleep together in your room. Remember, there was a time I shared it with you?"

I, who was now on my feet and getting into my nightgown, talked in an even, monotonous voice, in a voice I hoped sounded soothing and confident, about what a lovely idea that was, and how it was something we should definitely see to tomorrow, although I didn't think now was a good time to start, what with the lateness of the hour, our exhaustion, and my desire to go directly to sleep.

"Alma," he interrupted me suddenly, a note of concern—of apprehension—in his voice. "Isn't there something you're not telling me?"

"Not telling you?"

"Something in your heart, on your conscience . . ."

"What dear?"

He looked away for a full ten seconds, made a noise in his throat, then all of a sudden turned back to me and whispered: "Are you—?"

"What?"

"Laughing at me?"

"Rats, darling," I said softly. "Why would I laugh at you?"

"So then you're not laughing? You're not playing with me?"

"Why would I be playing with you?"

"And you still want me to move back in with you?"

"Why should I not? It will be wonderful, it has been wonderful. I wouldn't change my mind for anything."

My feelings of guilt, incidentally, although I had plenty of reasons to have them, seemed to have gotten lost in the imperative to exit his bedroom as quickly as possible. It was too late to tell the truth. Too late! Because Percy might already be in my room, wondering about my absence, growing impatient with it. It was now 11:05. Should Percy discover I had been with Rats, he could become furious. He could . . . Never mind, I did what I had to do, I told myself. I had to sleep with Rats. And now it's finished.

"Goodnight, Rats, I'm going."

"Goodnight to you then, my darling, but Alma . . ."

"Yes, Rats?"

"Aren't you going to say something else to me—something about moving back together?"

"We'll make arrangements for the move tomorrow. It can wait till tomorrow. Sweet dreams, darling, au revoir and remember, I love you."

I felt frenzied, frightened, and so hurried. I had not time to consider how I would be able to smooth my lies out later. I had time only to touch my lips to Rats' forehead, turn on my heels, and run upstairs.

12

Percy wasn't there, but I thought, just as well. I didn't want him to see me rushing into my room, breathless, my hair a mess, my skin greasy, perhaps, for all I knew, carrying Rats' scent. I felt as if I had just emerged from a swim in a pool of warm grease.

Quickly, I brushed my hair, brushed my teeth, rubbed a damp washcloth over my face and body, sprayed perfume all over myself.

But still I felt sticky and untidy. I felt that I could've spent the entire day in a steam bath and would've still felt unclean.

It was now eleven-thirty.

Where was Percy?

The one thing I knew I must not do is go prowling around the house looking for him. That would be suicide. I might run into Rats who'd ask who I was looking for, and he would recall that I told him I was exhausted and wanted to go directly to sleep. A degree of patience was essential. So I got into bed, put out the lamp, and with nothing to do but wait for Percy, experienced a reaction not only to all the effort with Rats but to all the tension of the last few days. Safe in my bed, the pressure off, I snuggled down into the side of the mattress where Percy usually slept, and went to sleep at once.

Only to be awakened by him when he climbed onto the bed. I remember becoming instantly wide awake when he got onto the bed next to me and also a feeling of alarm, a feeling that something was wrong, out of whack. I couldn't see him. The room was as dark as a dungeon but I could feel him. He was fully clothed. This was completely unlike him. He hadn't even taken his shoes off. I could smell him, too, an odd acidic smell, which was also uncharacteristic of him, and his body seemed very tense, tremulous.

Right away I said, "What's the matter, darling?" He said he was in trouble and could not tell me what it was, so I said, "Oh, you must tell me," and we went back and forth like this for two or three minutes, and then he said, "No, I don't think you could bear it, Alma." For a moment, I thought this had something to do with his mother, feeling only a sense of something more immediate, something more threatening, and then I said I was strong enough to bear anything. It was then he told me that he hurt Rats.

"Hurt Rats?" I repeated. "Hurt Rats?" My voice cracked, became high, quavering. I must have asked that several more times. Until finally, when he didn't answer my question, I answered it myself. "No, not true. You couldn't have hurt him." But even as I said that I knew that he had, some wordless part of myself knew that he was telling the truth, that he had done something horrible to Rats, and a cold wave spread over my body.

Percy breathed shakily, pressing the butt of his hand into his brow.

"Tell me what you did."

"I can't say it now."

"Yes, you can," I said. "You say it right now; you have to tell me; tell me or I'll be very angry with you."

He waited a beat or two. His voice was higher than usual, and thinner, nearly unrecognizable to me. "You're not going to like it."

He paused again as if giving me a chance to stop him. I remained silent and he said that when he discovered that I wasn't in my bedroom, he went downstairs, looking for me. When he saw me come out of Rats' study, he realized what had happened, that I had just had sexual intercourse with him.

"My first thought," he said, his voice beginning to tremble, "was of you and the baby, that I'd lose you both. But then it occurred to me that maybe I'd imagined the whole thing and that maybe I hadn't seen you come out of Rats' study at all and I was actually in bed dreaming. For some reason, I had the thought that maybe, if I walked out to the garden into the fresh air and acted as though I'd not seen you come out of Rats' study, then maybe, when I woke up later, I might find that you hadn't really slept with him. So I walked away from the study, feeling as though I was floating. I couldn't feel anything at all—except a slight dizziness and a desire to sleep. All my movements in fact felt like sleepwalking now—down the hall, out the front door, across the lawn. I was walking around the lawn, and did not know where I was going. Then I saw the tent that I had been putting up for Felix, the spikes, the mallet, and all of a sudden, my hand was gripping the mallet and pounding a spike into the ground. I stopped hammering and looked at the mallet. Then I carried it back to Rats' study, holding it in both my hands. As I entered the study, I saw him sitting up on his bed, and I stopped. 'What do you want now,' he said, seeing me. 'You have no business here. Get out of here.' At that point, I simply walked up to him and without thinking, lifted the mallet high up in the air and brought it down as hard as I could on the top of his head. I hit him two more times and then stepped back a pace, and looked at him, not thinking anything at all, except that I had done a bad thing and that you wouldn't be happy with me."

"Get under the covers, Percy," I said, helping him out of his trousers and shirt, and actually tucking him into the bed. "You're shivering."

"Alma," he said, "I'm sorry. I didn't want to do it. I don't know why I did it."

I stroked him to calm him. For some reason, the sight of his shivering, combined with his disconsolate and remorseful manner, helped me suppress panic. "You stay here. Don't come out of the bedroom until I tell you, do you understand?"

"Yes, Alma."

I remember feeling concerned about leaving him by himself but also feeling I had to see what he had done. To see whether what he had described was real or some kind of fantasy, to see whether there was some possibility of hope. Perhaps Percy *dreamed* he attacked Rats. He did say he thought he might've been in bed, sleeping. He told me all his movements felt like sleepwalking.

So, with my heart hammering, I put my robe on and ran downstairs. When I saw the door to Rats' study, which was slightly ajar, I found myself suddenly frozen, doubting my ability to move at all. I knew that something monstrous waited for me inside that room. The fact that the door was ajar, that Rats had not gotten up to close the door, seemed conclusive.

I stepped forward, peeked inside.

"Rats?"

No answer.

The silence seemed to expand inside me, the pressure building, as I stepped into the room and turned on the light. I tried to focus my eyes as the room went from blackness to almost surreal brightness and then suddenly I saw—the comforter on his bed piled in a heap, his head peeking out, his eyes now blue-black, swollen shut, the top of his head a mass of blood, of horror, blood matting his hair.

Hiding my eyes behind my fingers, I advanced in small steps. Then squatting beside the bed, the taste of bile rising to my mouth, I bent forward and stretched an arm toward the body.

"Rats," I said.

There was no response. But I knew he was still alive; leaning closer to get a better look, I saw that his chest was expanding and contracting, making a feeble, broken, desperate sound. I stood there looking at him, trying to sort out my thoughts, trying to think of what I should do next, but I just couldn't get beyond this dreamy, narcotic, light-headed feeling of disbelief and amazement. How was it possible? How was it possible that one minute ago he was healthy, his body thrumming with excitement, holding me to him with all his strength, and the next there was this mound of heavy mottled flesh? And that, suddenly, was all he was.

"*Irene!*" I shouted several times.

She came quickly turning white as a sheet as soon as her eyes took in the sight of the body on the bed. I'm not sure how long she stood there, looking at him, frozen in horror, but when she raised her eyes to look at me, her face twitched spasmodically, her hand went to her mouth and she took a couple of steps backwards, as though she thought I might spring at her, as though she thought I was the one who did this to him. And I couldn't then help imagining what others would think once they knew what she knew, what she must have known, which is that Percy and I were having an affair. We had a motive, they would think: two lovers in need of getting rid of the encumbrance, the woman's husband.

Spasms passed through my stomach, powerful, involuntary, as I tried to imagine how to explain to her that she was wrong, that it was just a horrible accident . . . but what kind of accident? In what kind of accident does a man get beaten over the head with a mallet?

So I just told—ordered—her to call the doctor.

Then I carefully propped Rats into a sitting position against the bed's headboard and ran to the bathroom. There seemed to be something wrong with leaving him by himself but I really had to go to the bathroom.

I knelt down and heaved in the toilet, rinsed my mouth, and then fetching a towel with a vague hope of dressing his wounds, returned to him and wrapped it around his limp floppy head, sorrow and guilt choking me:

Didn't you, didn't you do this to him? If you hadn't gotten involved with Percy, if you had been a better wife, a good wife—

But then, pulling away from him, in sudden hot rebellion against guilt, I remembered how he almost raped me, how cruel he had been to Felix, how he once said, on seeing Felix throw a ball, "For Christ sakes, do you have to throw it like a girl?" The great architect, the filthy beast of a father, how little he cared for his own son!

I was spurring myself on to a sort of contempt for the dying man but it was in vain. Because in the midst of trying to despise him, in the midst of trying to recall his many crudities, I couldn't take my eyes away from his battered bloodied body, barely breathing, looking almost as if his soul had deserted him, and I couldn't keep a new emotion from heaving to the surface—sadness. I began drowning in it. My brain became alive with images, sounds, voices, Rats' and mine commingled, of our last moments together: the sad stubborn expression on his face when he told me he couldn't sleep without me, his sad brown eyes, how absurdly excited I became while trying to get him to sleep with me, how surprised and excited he was to see and feel my excitement, the weight of his body on mine, the sound of his breathing, his groan at climax, the sigh when he curled his back against mine, spooning. And without quite understanding why, I found myself rocking him back and forth, hugging him with an ardor that almost amounted to delirium.

So that when Dr. O'Donnell, a slight balding old Irishman with a stethoscope around his neck, entered the room and stood over me, he had to tap me on the shoulder to get my attention.

Would I make a little room, he asked, so he could examine the patient.

There was an interval of stillness and concentration as he felt Rats' pulse, examined his wounds, and carefully looked into his eyes. Then he knelt down beside me, eye level (I was now sitting on the floor beside Rats' bed), and asked me what happened to my husband.

I could hear his assistant speaking to Irene in the study, their whispers like a smooth, satiny murmur in the background.

"Madam?"

What? I stared at him, wondering what on earth could be going through his head, what suspicions and judgments were being entertained. I had no idea how to do this, what to tell him. I felt like I was going mad.

"Madam, I am asking a simple question."

Something about the entire situation—the shock and the sordidness of it, and of course, the sadness, but also the fact that it was Percy who did this and that he never would have if I hadn't seduced him—froze my tongue. I couldn't get words out. Watch what you say, I kept telling myself. Over the last few months, you took pleasure in Percy's body. You enjoyed him immensely. Love you called it. How can you now repay him by identifying him as the murderer? It isn't your responsibility to blame him. It's your responsibility to deflect blame *from* him.

But how, I wanted to know. What should I do? What story should I tell?

"Can you tell me anything, Mrs. Rattenbury, anything at all?"

Finally, I took a breath and just asked, "What do you want to know?"

"The"—Dr. O'Donnell hesitated—"the wounds, madam, the injuries. How were they inflicted? Can you tell me anything?"

He did not wait for me to reply but instead got to his feet and looked at me coldly and mistrustfully. "Well, I'm afraid there isn't much I can do for him anyway." All he could do at this point, he said, is telephone a surgeon and attempt to obtain a second opinion. Then he excused himself to make the call.

Alone again with my husband, I looked to the decanter of sherry, now somewhat less than half-full, still on his nightstand. I needed a drink before I faced the doctor again, before I let another minute go by, and without consciously deciding to, got up and seized the decanter, gulping down one swallow after another, almost emptying it. I was more than a little lightheaded by the time the doctor returned and asked me if I had any idea why someone might have assaulted my husband. Had I been in a condition to exercise a soberer judgment and seen things objectively, had I only realized the utter transparency of my position and how ludicrous, immoral, and unfeeling it appeared, I might very well have told him what Percy told me. But I was not at all sober and a most bizarre strategy flashed into my mind: the idea that perhaps Rats' injuries could be seen as self-inflicted.

I jumped to my feet, stumbled over to Rats' nightstand where I seized the book he had been reading, *Stay of Execution.* I showed it to the doctor. "Could my husband—" I cleared my throat. "Could he have gotten the idea of suicide from this book? Is that a possibility?"

He shook his head and smiled derisively at me. "Mrs. Rattenbury, a self-inflicted wound is out of the question."

I stared at him a few moments and considered reading to him the excerpt that Rats had read to me but then thought better of it as I didn't know what page it was on; besides, it wouldn't have made any difference.

"There were three blows to the head, each sufficient to knock him unconscious," he said and stopped. "I'm sorry, Mrs. Rattenbury, but you will probably need to make a statement to the police."

My knees gave. The room spinning, I collapsed to the floor, as much, I think, from the bewilderment as from fear. It had all happened too fast, this sudden out-of-the-blue cataclysm. I had no idea how to deal with any of it.

"Have they been called?" I asked.

"Yes," he said and kneeled beside me again, putting his hand on my brow looking at me with a kindly expression. He said I should elevate my legs and lay down, and said that I was probably in a state of shock.

I let him help me to my feet and lead me to the drawing room where I stretched out on the divan. I covered my eyes with my forearm, and because I was so tired, I immediately fell asleep. My sleep was very light; it was a tissue. If I wanted I could blow it away. I wanted to; I wanted to blow it away, so I could keep abreast of everything that was happening. But when I opened them and glanced at the clock, I saw it was one-thirty. An hour had passed. How could it be possible? I couldn't have slept that long. Then I felt something or someone stroking my cheek. It seemed impossible that anyone would stroke my cheek, that anyone would be tender to me. I turned my head; Irene was standing beside the divan.

"Hello, darling," I said.

"How are you managing, Alma?"

I tried to smile. "I suppose I've had better nights."

"Let me see you upstairs. You can't be comfortable here. Can I help you get into your own bed?"

I sat up and looked around, feeling rather disoriented, and asked why the house was so quiet, where everyone had gone.

She explained that the surgeon had been here; he saw at once that Rats was in a critical condition but found it impossible to make a proper examination in the house. So he called an ambulance and made arrangements for the operating theater to be prepared at Strathallen Nursing Home on Wharnclife Road. Moments later he left in his car to prepare the instruments. Dr. O'Donnell followed with Rats in the ambulance.

We walked in silence to the stairs, with her arm around me. And then I turned to her because I had to say what I hoped, with every fiber, she'd tell me was false.

"Rats is dying."

"Yes," she said. "I know."

And then it resurfaced, the feeling of sadness. I pulled away from Irene and yanked at my hair, overwhelmed by the need to do something to relieve my pain right away, yet without any idea what that thing was. I began jerking my head back and forth, right and left, as if searching for a way out, an answer. "What am I going to do? What am I going to do?" I kept asking.

"Alma," I heard her say, "whatever happened to Rats is out of your hands. It's not your responsibility. You don't have to do anything except take care of yourself."

And she put her arm around me once again and began leading me up the stairs. We climbed the first four or five. Then, I stopped. Suddenly, from nowhere, the decision came.

"Not my responsibility?" I said, staring at her and gripping her very hard by the shoulders. "What would you say if I told you that it is? What would you say if I told you that I did it?"

It came out just like that. I did it! Well, yes, why not? Why ever not? I'm stronger than Percy. I can carry this load; I'm an adult. Percy's just a boy. He hasn't done anything with his life; he hasn't lived or traveled or had an education. And anyway, my conscience wouldn't let me not assume responsibility. I should be held responsible and I was going to be held responsible and to hell with what anybody thinks.

"I don't believe you," Irene said, staring at me with a look of wonder on her face. "Not for a moment. You would never hurt anyone."

"Listen," I said. I had not planned any of this but I could feel the idea flowing into my brain and almost before I knew it I had the whole story, the whole absurd confession, worked out clearly in my head. "I'm terribly, terribly sorry to disappoint you, darling, but you're wrong about me. I'm perfectly capable of hurting someone if I feel it's the right thing. Did you know that Rats has been suicidal for a very long time? He said he couldn't go on living; life had become intolerable to him. I hit him over the head with the mallet because he begged me. Because he said he'd do it himself if I didn't help him. I didn't have a choice."

Did she believe me? Would I believe me, if I were she?

Her chin went up and she was staring down at me along the full length of her nose. "I know what you're trying to do, Alma. You're saying that to cover for Percy."

"This has nothing to do with Percy—"

She snapped, "I won't let you do this to yourself, Alma—"

"This has nothing to do with Percy," I snapped back, "and if you tell people otherwise, I'll tell them you're only trying to protect me. We're best friends and you'd say anything to help me."

"And what about Felix? You would leave him motherless?"

She was trying to make me feel guilty. How shallow she was, how foolishly lacking in insight! She might have been speaking to me in a foreign language, in Swahili, when she started talking to me about my son. That's how far off the mark she was. "Thank you, Irene, but I know what I'm doing."

"Why do you want to make him an orphan?"

"If you'll excuse me, I'm going to go to bed now. I'm very tired."

She looked at me, and then turned away to take a handkerchief from her pocket and blow her nose. It was as though I was no longer there. And suddenly, everything I had just said seemed appalling and foolish. I had not thought anything through. My thought about assuming the blame had been a half-formed impulse, not a plan for action. I did not really know what the police would do with me. Would I be arrested and prosecuted for attempted murder? Would I be sent to prison? Lose my son? Lose my home? Overturn every element of what I currently call my life? Perhaps. And yet I believed—although I could not explain why—that it was the right decision.

Irene turned back to me after she put her handkerchief in her pocket. I could see the restraint in her face as she tried to hold back her sharp condemnation. "What does it matter what I believe?" she said. "What does anything matter? I can't convince you to change your mind, now can I?"

I could feel the tears pricking at my eyes. "I'm so sorry, Irene—"

"It's all right."

"I'm a foolish woman, you know. I made mistakes. I've hurt people. If I've hurt you, I apologize."

"You're hurting me now."

"All I can say is, I'm sorry," I said and kissed her, and then I turned away and headed up the stairs.

13

It was almost two o'clock when I sat down beside him on the bed and shook his shoulder. He had been asleep.

He woke with a small cry, almost like a cough, and then reached up and touched my cheek.

"Want to lie down," he said, pulling away the covers, making a space for me. "Here," he said.

"This isn't the time," I said.

"For just a moment."

Perhaps it was his touch—when he reached out his hands and gently gripped me above the elbows—or perhaps his warm sleepy smell. I no longer remember what, if anything precisely, made me forget Rats and forget my decision, but by the time he put his head next to mine and I felt his fevered cheek, my thought processes ceased. How could this skin-and-bone stripling once again overcome my better judgment? By weariness, I suppose, and too much sherry. And down I went, collapsing into his arms, all at once aware of the heaviness, the weariness of my limbs. Nothing in my sense of decency, nothing in my character, seemed capable of marshalling resistance. So why try? Why pretend I didn't want him? Why pretend I didn't want to leave this terrifying dream behind, to lift with him, to fly, to fly, to fly far away on that body and in those arms? And for a few moments, it actually seemed as though there was no wounded husband, no doctors, no police, nothing but Percy and me with our arms around each other—oh, far more than that—fairly clinging to each other with fear and desire. It was as if we wanted to devour each other with kisses.

I hadn't considered the possibility that these would be our last kisses. Had I known, I might have enjoyed them. Or perhaps I did enjoy them but my guilt would not allow me to admit it to myself. For when a wave of disbelief swept over me, I disengaged myself and sat up, shivering with disgust. "Mother of God!" I said as Rats' face flashed into my mind, his face bruised and clotted with blood, blood everywhere. "What's the matter with me? How could I be making love with you now . . . with Rats on the surgeon's table?"

He scarcely reacted. I wondered if he understood. I put the lamp on and looked at him—the soft curves of his cheek, the tousled hair that now fell over his eyes. How innocent he looked! There was something almost shocking about the sweetness of his features. Then I shook my head from side to side as a dark idea reared its head, the idea that he hadn't once thought of *me*. Not once had he thought of me as someone to turn to, or talk to, and not once thought of me as someone who would be damaged by this explosion of his, my whole life in ruins. Who are you, I thought, and how could you? And in a vague sort of way, I wondered whether there was something wrong with him, something I'd missed, something I didn't understand, that he was not the person I thought he was.

"Percy," I said, "How can you make love to me, after you've—" I sighed rather than name the thing he had done. "You're not out of your mind, are you?"

Now he was sitting up; now he was facing me. I could feel his hands on my waist, asking me to fall back onto the bed with him.

I shuddered. "Forgive me for this, Percy. But I don't understand anything." All at once I was picturing him battering Rats with a mallet. At the same time, still disbelieving, still telling myself it was impossible, that he couldn't have done this. "Do you know what you're doing? Did you know what you were doing when you—"

"I already told you. It wasn't something I planned. I didn't want to hurt him."

"But you did."

"Yes."

"How could you, how could you call yourself sane after you've done something like *that*?"

"Oh, Alma." His arms tightened around me, and again he pulled me toward the bed.

"Don't," I said. "I'm asking how could you?"

He sat up straight and put his hands to his face, then ran them through his hair. "It was because he made love with you—"

"You're saying you were jealous? Good heavens, was that your only reason—"

"*No, Alma!* It was not my only reason. Take it easy, will you. The baby you're carrying is mine and I couldn't bear the idea that he'd assume it was his, that he'd take it away—"

"Yes . . . yes . . . all right. But when you knew . . . when I told you I had decided to make him believe he was the father, when I told you I was going to sleep with him"—I shuddered again—"and you knew you couldn't accept it, why didn't you leave? You said you wanted to go to school in London. It would have been easy for you. Why didn't you just leave?"

"Yes, I suppose I should have."

"So why didn't you? Why, oh why, didn't you just quit?"

"I honestly didn't think about it more than once or twice. Anyway, what does it matter now? It won't undo what's already done."

He got off the bed and looked out the window and I was startled again at how his ribs jutted out, somehow infinitely touching, like a starving fawn.

I asked, "Has it occurred to you that someone might see you?"

He shrugged apathetically, retreated a few steps, rested his head against the wall and closed his eyes.

"And has it occurred to you the police will be here in minutes?"

He didn't seem to find the question worthy of an answer. He just walked back to the foot of the bed where he retrieved his clothing and began dressing—although a moment later, while tying his shoelaces, something must have finally penetrated. His eyes narrowed and he looked at me, and asked, "The police will be here in minutes? Is that what you said?"

"Yes."

"What are we going to tell them?" he asked. "What are we going to do?"

This was my opening, the moment to share my plan. But before I had a chance to organize my thoughts and tell him what I'd decided, he answered his own question with a slight shrug, shaking his head. "I suppose we don't really have to do anything. There's really nothing we can do. I'll be arrested. It's not very complicated."

I thought of flinging back at him, "Oh, yes, it is, it's very complicated. It's complicated because I've decided to take the blame," but I again hesitated. I suppose I must have known he wouldn't hear of it, known he would have called the whole idea absurd, and known there was nothing I could say that would make him think otherwise, so I just said, stupidly, "Why must you insist on simplifying everything?"

He stared at me. "Simplifying what? What are you talking about? I attacked Rats without provocation. I have no defense. That's all there is. It's over."

I felt a need to hold onto this thought, to try to understand it. *It's over.* But then I heard the sound of car doors slamming, voices, footsteps on the gravel—the police?—and it was erased like chalk from a blackboard. I was suddenly too ill-at-ease to carry on this conversation, now longing desperately to get dressed, and get away from him. "Can't you move any faster," I hissed, "you've got to get out of here right now—*now.*"

There is not much else to tell. As he left the room, his shirt-tail hanging out, he told me he loved me, but I ignored him, feeling curiously as if I was watching this scene instead of being a part of it, that it belonged not to my life, but another's, a mood which followed me downstairs when I greeted the visitors: six officers of the law carrying weapons, but none threatening me, six messengers of peace with smooth and boyish faces beneath their narrow-brimmed hats. I had been expecting something apocalyptic. But the police—or wine, I couldn't tell you which, though I suppose it was the latter—seemed to have the most reassuring effect on me. I watched myself, surprised, at how suddenly I didn't seem frightened or tired anymore. I seemed to be feeling, in fact, a weird euphoria, amazed at how easy it was to mingle and how kind everyone was treating me. Everyone was polite. Everyone smiled. Everyone was more than grateful for another tumbler of Scotch. And for the remainder of the night I went about pouring drinks, and saying this and saying that, not caring what I said, thinking nothing mattered except that I take the blame for assaulting Rats.

I'm told I put records on the gramophone, laughed hysterically, danced around, and at one point even tried to kiss one of the detectives. I made a complete fool of myself, words flying from my mouth like wood chips from a buzz saw. Not a good time to be behaving in such a manner, the worst possible time, because the police were taking statements from everyone.

A handsome young inspector named Bagwell, the one I tried to kiss, was alone with Irene and me when I suddenly announced, "I know who did it!"

Out came his pencil and notebook.

"I did it with a mallet."

"Where is the mallet?"

"It is hidden," I said, and then, for some reason, added, "It is urine on the chair." I don't actually remember saying that but I'm told that is what I did say, and I'm told this is when Dr. O'Donnell returned from the operating theater to inform us that Rats had died, and to tell Bagwell that I was not in a condition to make a statement, and that I needed to go to bed to sleep the alcohol off. The only other thing I really remember is my feeling of loyalty to Percy, and my decision, my plan: Let them do to me what they want, but if he is charged, all is lost; even if they only discover the truth about our relationship, all is still lost.

14

So that appalling night passed. My drinking forced it to end and I was led to my bedroom, only to be awakened the following morning at about seven by three detectives. They told me to get up. I told them to leave me alone. The sunlight was excruciating. It cut into the room like so many yellow knives—reflecting on the windows and draperies and cushions and finally entering the brittle skull and throbbing consciousness of the worst hangover I had ever experienced.

The detectives told Irene to make some coffee and then they propped me up and made me drink it. I could barely hold the cup. For ten or possibly fifteen minutes, the detectives stood leaning against the wall in silence, throwing embarrassed glances at me, their faces appearing angular and inhuman, the only sounds the sparrows that nested in the high corners of the house, until finally Irene protested, "The lady can't get up with three men in her room. Give her a chance!"

Two detectives left but one remained, a short man with straight brick-colored hair and tired red-rimmed eyes. He said he had been ordered not to let me out of his sight but would turn around. I got dressed as quickly as possible. Meanwhile, a new inspector, a man of about forty, rather tall, thin, with an exceedingly agreeable face—unmistakably Welsh—came into the room. I did not know his name then, nor did I ever see him again, but I christened him "the interrogator." He asked me to explain my relationship with Percy.

"He is my chauffeur," I said.

"You're having an affair with him?"

"No."

"What sort of relationship do the two of you have?"

"We have a cordial relationship."

"What do you do together?"

"As I said, he is the chauffeur. He drives the car."

The interrogator scribbled something on a pad, then nodded. "Why don't you tell me the truth about your relationship?"

I said I already had.

The interrogator sounded weary. "Everyone knows you're having an affair with him," he said. "You know that that's what everyone says."

"I've heard that before."

He nodded his head, exasperated. "Yes, yes. But is it the truth?"

I shook my head. "It isn't."

The interrogator leaned forward and stared at me intently. "You're having an affair with Percy Stoner. The two of you planned to murder your husband."

"That's untrue. I am not having an affair with him. And we did not plan to murder my husband."

We went through this basic set of questions two more times. The interrogator asked the same questions; I gave the same answers. After the third go-round, another inspector came into the bedroom and asked the interrogator to confer with him in the hallway. When the two of them returned, the interrogator announced that they had made a critical discovery in the garden—the mallet—and were now in a position to charge that I did "grievous bodily harm to one Francis Mawson Rattenbury in an attempt to murder him on Sunday, the third of November, 1934."

Irene was looking directly at me, a stricken expression on her face. She looked like death itself. I tried to smile at her and took her hand, and sought for something funny or lighthearted to say, but she pulled away, saying, "Oh, it can't be true. Oh, dear God no!"

"I'm so sorry, Irene."

You're probably imagining I felt wretched at this moment, and of course, I was, I was absolutely desolate, but there was also a way in which I felt exalted.

They say each of us needs a purpose in life—it is a fundamental property of human nature—and that our main challenge as humans is to find the right one. Well, for me that morning that challenge had been settled. My purpose was to shield Percy. That, no doubt, was all I had but it was something I could really get my teeth into, just as Percy had gotten his teeth into me. At that moment I cared about nothing else. On that morning, in my bedroom, while the interrogator fired his questions at me, while my head throbbed and the other inspectors stared, their faces cold, seeming inhuman, and I felt cold and inhuman; on that morning, when there seemed no shred of dignity left to me, when it seemed I was the lowliest creature to inhabit the earth, lower than a bottom-feeding crustacean, I still believed in a principle that redeemed my life and gave it meaning: *I will do anything I have to, to keep Percy out of this, to protect him— anything.* And so I narrowed my eyes and looked at the interrogator and turned up the butane on my Canadian accent. "Oh, to hell with it!" I said. "Let's end this thing now, eh? If I'm guilty, I'm guilty. It's all the same, eh?"

This was the story I gave: "About eleven p.m. on Sunday, the third of November, 1934, I was reading to my husband in his study when he dared me to kill him as he wanted to die. I picked up the mallet. He then said, 'You have not got the guts to do it.' I then hit him with the mallet. I hid the mallet outside the house. I would have shot him if I had had a gun."

I asked to see what the interrogator had written. He showed me his notebook. The words danced before my eyes, and for a moment I thought, what have I done! I was amazed at myself. Then I started to fret about whether or not I should have first consulted with my solicitor. I fretted still more when it occurred to me that one of the penalties for murder is hanging. But I was not entirely concerned. For once in my life, I thought, I was doing something redemptive, something pure. Didn't I deserve to be punished for seducing Percy? Shouldn't I make it possible for him to live a normal happy life, as though he had never met me? Yes, of course, I should. And so, feeling proud of my moral courage and my cool decisiveness, rather like a terminally ill cancer patient writing her will, detailing her assets and leaving them all to charity, I read the statement aloud and signed it.

15

What had I gotten myself into? What indeed? And why, later that day, did my self-sacrificial haze evaporate? Why, after I was taken to the Bournemouth Police Station and locked in a cell, did I change my mind and tell the truth? Why did I say, "Percy murdered Rats"?

For one thing, I thought of Felix. I know it sounds strange that I would confess to a murder I didn't commit, allow myself to be arrested and imprisoned, without once thinking of him. Yes, it is strange, too strange to imagine, but it's true. I didn't think about him until I was alone in my cell and then I thought about him continually: *Would it be fair to him to allow myself to be imprisoned as a sacrifice to Percy? Felix has all his life before him. Is he to be known as the son of a woman who murdered his father? Do I have the right to blast his life to bits to shield my lover? Don't I owe it to him to tell the whole truth?*

And what about Percy himself, would he let me sacrifice myself for him? Impossible! He would never allow it. Hadn't he said he had no defense? Hadn't he said he expected to be charged and convicted? Yes, sacrificing my life for his might have been a brave idea, a virtuous idea, but it was an impractical one. He would come forward. He would tell the truth. So what would my false confession accomplish? Claiming I murdered Rats would only help the prosecution hang me, without benefit of saving him.

Now it becomes necessary to reveal something rather shameful and embarrassing about myself. I may not have been entirely straightforward in the recital of my motivation. I claimed that I confessed to murdering my husband in order to shield Percy, a worthy motivation, perhaps, but it now seems to me there is something else I was attempting to accomplish. And that something else is this: I was hoping to conceal our affair. I am saying maybe it wasn't only that I didn't want him to be accused of the murder; maybe it's that I didn't really want Percy's reasons for committing the murder—his jealousy of Rats and my pregnancy—publicized.

Why would I risk getting hanged to conceal an affair that everyone apparently already knew about? Why foster the impression that I was a murderer, and risk turning my son into an orphan, in the vague hope of withholding final confirmation of a seedy little liaison? Why, oh why, indeed? These are good questions, and I cannot say how many hours I laid on my cot staring through my barred windows, pondering them. Was it that I feared humiliation more than prison? Would I rather go to prison than be turned into a source of bargain-basement entertainment? Did I imagine prison would be my last barrier of defense against becoming turned into an object of salacious fascination? (I was certain people would find my sexual adventures hideously amusing.)

I don't know; I can only say that for a while, however briefly, I believed it would be far better to go to prison than tell the truth. That's what I believed while I was still in my own house; what I believed before they locked me into the steel-and-concrete cell that had a barred arched window at one end and at the other a heavy door with a sliding panel with a round observation hole above it; what I believed before I heard the observation panel slide open and realized that a warder or someone—I really had no idea who—was now observing me, and could observe me at any time; what I believed until I felt my stomach rise to my throat and I threw myself down on the cold stone floor in the darkest corner of my cell and heard myself praying wildly for God to help me, curling myself into a ball in a desperate effort to hide.

I had read descriptions of prisons in books—I had seen prison movies—and it all seemed like a game. After getting locked up, however, I realized it was not a game. I asked one of the warders why I had to be observed through the hole in my door. He said it was to make sure I didn't hang myself. All right, I said, very well, but was it possible that whoever was intending to look through my peep hole could first knock so I could at least have a moment of warning while dressing or using the slop bucket? He did not laugh, but with a face twisted by fierce disgust, he threw at me, "This isn't your home; this is a jail and you happen to be on suicide watch." And it was exactly this refrain that I heard repeated by all the warders: this isn't your home, this is a jail, and you have no rights whatsoever. You are entitled to nothing.

I was not entitled to shoes. They have nails in them. Slippers were what I had to wear. Knives, forks, and ceramic dishes were forbidden too, as were pencils. Books were forbidden too. Did you know that books have a small piece of wire in the binding, which can be used to cut flesh? I wasn't allowed matches either. I might self-immolate. When I wanted a cigarette, a warder had to light it for me.

Imagine a woman who has lost her privacy, lost her shoes, lost her home, lost her books, lost her son, lost her husband and lover, all lost together, at the very same moment. Imagine how she feels.

She feels death is preferable.

You see, the story of the heroic woman torn between her great and protective love for her young lover and her maternal love for her son, finally giving way to her stronger maternal instincts, is false, or rather, incomplete. I didn't see any point to remaining in prison, and didn't want to hurt Felix, but it is also true that I felt threatened, besieged at every moment in these new quarters. I reacted to prison with panic from the very start. I felt as though I was becoming hollowed out, I feared I'd soon forget who I was, and I believed that if they released me, my unspeakable debasement would end.

How mistaken I was.

Three days after my arrest and two days after Percy's (he was arrested after I identified him as the murderer), they took us to the Bournemouth courthouse for arraignment where laborers, shopkeepers, office workers, mothers and children were lying in wait for us. I couldn't have been more exposed if I had been sentenced to stand on a platform in a public square and had my ear nailed to the post of a pillory. But the press said I had murdered my husband and slept with my chauffeur, who was nothing more than a lad, and so I had to be gazed at, jeered, execrated, and pelted with mud. I am not exaggerating when I tell you that the people milling around the courthouse went into a frenzy the moment they saw me. Not one face showed the slightest sign of normal human feeling, the faintest hint of sympathy. People were pushing and shoving each other, leaning out of windows and doorways, standing on the tops of cars, on fenders and running boards, standing on tiptoe, hissing and cursing, piercing the air with laughter and shrieks. "There she is, the filthy adulteress!" "You're going to hang for this, you whore! You're going to swing!" This from a red-faced farm boy who leaned forward, his mouth only inches from mine, as I was getting out of the car: "You dirty rotten bimbo—you murderer! You thought you'd get away with it, didn't you?" Even the police, who were there to keep order, seemed to be on tiptoe too, craning their necks on the chance of catching sight of me. What could they hope to see? Lucretia Borgia, Medusa, Messalina, Lady Macbeth, Jezebel? At the very least, a woman who is old, ugly, exhausted. I tried to think of something beautiful, something spiritual and artistic, something to take my mind away, to arouse tender feelings and noble sentiments, but nothing came to me—nothing except shame. The shame—is there anything on earth more terrible, more soul-destroying to a woman?

What shamed me most was the perception that I had abandoned Percy, whom I loved all the more for having led into this nightmare, and even more than that, for having informed on him. How can I describe what it was like to see him at the arraignment, sitting at the opposite end of the courtroom, dressed in his gray suit and blue tie—his chauffeur uniform— his hair neatly brushed back, his eyes swollen with grief, never turning to make a gesture to me, to look at me, as though I was invisible to him, not once attempting to defend himself or cast any doubt that he alone hammered the fatal blows? Had he given up? Could he have given up because he thought I had abandoned him? Did he think I had betrayed him? And might those thoughts, if he had them, somehow push him over the edge? Might he hurt himself or go mad knowing he was on his own, all the responsibility for the murder now on his narrow shoulders?

I can only tell you that the need to explain myself to him, combined with the impossibility of doing so, felt like being buried alive. I would have done anything for a friendly look from him, a smile.

And so, yes, I told the truth, I told the magistrates what Percy told me the night he murdered Rats, hammering a stake into his heart, without gaining any advantage for myself. I was still charged with murder despite the fact that at the arraignment, Percy testified that he had murdered Rats on his own, without any help from me. He'd killed Rats, he said, because he had taken two heaped-up tablespoons of cocaine. He said he found the drug at his father's house and was temporarily deranged. Innocent by virtue of insanity was his plea, a defense that was laughable, totally beyond belief, since he didn't even know what the drug looked like. A brownish substance with dark specks, that's how he described it to one of the doctors.

Still, he did confess to the crime. Wouldn't you think that after the magistrates heard him say he struck the murder blows, they would've released me? But no, not at all: the prosecution contended, and the board of magistrates seemed to believe, it was immaterial who actually wielded the mallet. It was immaterial since the murder was probably a joint agreement, a lover's conspiracy. As one senior barrister for the prosecution argued, his mouth twisted into a contemptuous smile, "The evidence will clearly show that the relationship between the accused was not confined to that usually expected between a lady and her servant," as if proving Percy and I were lovers could alone establish a conspiracy to murder. So even if I managed to prove that I was absent from the murder scene, the prosecution intended to find me guilty as an accessory before the fact by demonstrating that I had advised him, encouraged him, counseled, aided and abetted.

All I gained by telling the truth was the additional burden that I was responsible for Percy's arrest. I may have had every reason to believe he would have eventually come forward and confessed on his own, but the fact is, he did not. I named him as the killer and the police stormed into his bedroom and arrested him before he said a word to anyone.

16

After the arraignment, my counsel, M. T. O'Connor, came to my cell; a short, pot-bellied rumpled man with dark intense eyes and thick dark brows. He had a question for me. Irene told him that on the murder night I spent a lot of time alone with Rats in his study. Could I explain to him what was going on there?

I looked down at my hands for a moment, picturing Irene seeing me go into Rats' study. "It was crazy, I know that," I said. "I wanted to give our marriage another try, and I just didn't give enough thought to Percy, to how he might respond."

O'Connor's face firmed, suddenly looking graver, more focused. "Are you saying you slept with your husband that night and that Percy knew it?"

I nodded.

"I see," he said and jotted something down on his pad. Then he asked how I knew that Percy knew.

I explained that Percy told me he saw me come out of Rats' study, which he used as a bedroom. What I was thinking was: *Maybe I shouldn't be telling him this.*

Seeing the concern on my face, O'Connor changed his tone. "No need to worry," he said, rubbing his hands together and winking slightly. "There is no way a jury could convict you of conspiracy to murder." Conspiracy requires deliberation, he explained, but was there any evidence of deliberation here? The method of murder was the clumsiest method that could be devised. There was no thought of masking the crime, no thought of making the death seem accidental, and no thought of establishing an alibi. Was there any chance of escape? None. Who would plan a murder like that?

That wasn't what I had been worrying. I had of course been worrying whether O'Connor might somehow use what I'd just told him—that Percy knew I'd slept with Rats—to harm Percy's defense. But then he kept rattling on about how good my chances of being acquitted were and I put my fear for Percy out of my head. I didn't even question him when he told me that Percy would be taken to Dorchester Prison and I would be taken to Women's Prison at Holloway in North London, and that I should prepare myself for the fact that we would not be allowed to communicate with one another. I made up my mind then that whatever happened to Percy was out of my hands, and that all I could do was hope against hope he was well and all right, and try to live and survive as best I could on my own, without worrying about him. I made all sorts of sensible resolutions: I would push away any thought of him; I would pretend he didn't exist; yes, pretend he didn't exist, that was essential.

Just the same, when I got to Holloway, I thought about little else. In a way that I find hard to explain, his very absence made him seem more real, my memory of him more acute. His touch, his voice, his scent, all came back to me. At nightfall, under the covers, I'd imagine him beside me, his fingers touching my eyebrows, bringing to me another night—when I woke to the feel of his fingers on my brow and him asking me: "Whose eyebrows are these?" I replied: "Mine." "Oh, no," he said laughing, "they belong to me." Or the night he woke me, supporting himself on an elbow, to ask if he could share his dream: "I dreamed there was a new law. It was now against the law to wear a mask; all the masks had to be burned." Or on a sunny morning, writing in my journal, I'd suddenly find myself entranced and motionless, seeing in front of me not the white paper but the white shining teeth, his head tilted back in laughter, his eyes assuming almost the same shape and size as his mouth. Or scrubbing my cell in the afternoon, my heart would race, because he might come up behind me—remembering so clearly the time he surprised me when I was scrubbing the car, the day he traced an A on my back with a wet finger, and then kissed me at the tip of the letter, just below my neck. *"I feel we're some sort of assembly line—a car-washing team,"* he had said.

Such was my state of mind while I lived in Holloway. I thought about our former happiness constantly, and the more I thought about our happy times together, the more I missed them, and the more I hated this life behind bars: hated that the warders could observe me at any moment without warning; hated the slop bucket in my cell, especially that it had no lid; hated being locked in my solitary cell for twenty-three out of every twenty-four hours, which to my mind is a cruel and unusual punishment; hated the moisture that condensed on the stone walls of my cell and ran down to the floor; hated that I was forced to wear what the prison staff called the "standard outfit" which included coarse brown panties that resemble men's boxer shorts. Above all, I hated the food. On Christmas day we were given a boiled chicken leg, a badly cooked potato, six ounces of beans, six ounces of fig and suet pudding, and told we had been allotted these luxuries through the generosity of His Majesty and the Church of England, and should be most grateful. I wanted to hurl it; I simply wanted to kill the smiling warder who informed me of my obligation to feel grateful.

There is a sort of desperation that takes hold of a woman in prison, a dreadful feeling of the world's condemnation, not only of her crime, but also of her whole being and everyone connected to her. My son, for example; he came to see me at Hol-

loway, during my second week. Irene brought him. We met in
the visitors' room, a large square-shaped room with warders
standing watch at the corners. I sat on one side of a large oak
table and they sat on the other, a high iron grill separating us.
On my side of the table were a half dozen other prisoners,
prostitutes for the most part. On the visitors' side were
prisoners' family and friends, boyfriends and pimps. I counted
four or five other small children and they were making a lot of
noise. They all seemed to be talking at once; everyone was quite
loud. I was embarrassed that Felix should see me in this
company and see me wearing the brown prison uniform. I felt
dirty and unkempt, deserving every punishment that had come
my way or ever would again, and Felix looked angry. I was
startled by how sullen he looked. He sat behind Irene, hunched
over, watching me.

"When are you coming home?" he asked. His voice sounded
high, stressed.

"I'm coming home very soon, darling." I spoke with a smile.
I tried to make my expression look happy, confident. "I'll be
bringing you lots of presents. I miss you very much."

On both sides of us, a Babel of voices shouted messages. One
of the women visitors stared at me and then elbowed her
companion: *She's that Rattenbury woman, you know, the one having the affair with her chauffeur.*

Is that what she said? Could I have been imagining?

Felix looked at Irene. "What did Mommy say?" he asked.
"This place, it's too noisy here."

"I said I miss you very much," I shouted.

"Tell Mommy you miss her too," Irene said.

He didn't speak; he just looked at Irene.

"Go ahead, tell her you miss her too," Irene nudged. "Just
speak up, darling."

At this point Felix tugged at Irene's hand—with an urgency

that I would try without success to forget—begging her to take him out of there. Irene looked at me. She looked absolutely miserable. "This hasn't been a good day for him. You know, this isn't easy for him."

"I know," I said, feeling a quick anger, a kind of hatred for my son who was uncomfortable visiting this place where I was forced to live, and then a kind of internal tremor. I felt I was failing a critical test. I began to feel I ought to be asking him questions: about school, about his friends. I ought to be joking; I ought to be making him laugh. But my mind had gone blank. I turned around, trying to hide. All the shame, the noise, the squalor, the long waiting and disappointment, cut my heart in two, and for the moment, the idea of getting away from them became the only thing on my mind. I turned to face them again. "It's too hard to talk in here," I said. "I just can't do it."

Next thing I was out the door, into the corridor, around the corner and back in my cell. For a moment, I considered chewing my wrists, severing my arteries. Damn it, damn it, *damn* it. I banged the fleshy edge of my hand against the steel bars in my window. Then I threw myself down on my cot, burying my head beneath my arms. I tried to think of horses, to imagine myself riding across fields and open country. But thoughts of Felix kept intruding. I could not stop thinking of him. I imagined he was in the cell with me, playing with his toys, his toy soldiers spread all over the floor, his sweet little voice humming songs, his hand in mine. And then, in the midst of this fantasy, I thought he did not need a mother like me. I am a curse to him. And there fell on me this almost unbearable pain—perhaps longing is the word for it, a longing not to be the woman or the mother I am, and I bade farewell to everybody and everything dear to me: Felix, Percy, husband, home, friends, music. I wanted to die.

And that evening, I thought I was, in fact, dying. Three or

four hours after I walked away from Felix, there was a sudden explosion of blood and tissue. I didn't at first understand that this was a miscarriage. And when I did, while I sat on my slop bucket, waiting for the bleeding to stop, my feelings were violently mixed. The pain was searing, and I felt ashamed and loathsome, but it was also the end of something shameful and loathsome. I hated being pregnant, and hated that I couldn't tell anyone. It was worse in prison than at home, because at home at least there was some privacy, there was some control over my life. Now I was living in a cage. I was like a zoo animal.

This was not, of course, the way I imagined the pregnancy would end, fearing the blood might never stop, fearing I might bleed to death, and fearing the warders' questions. But at least it was an end; it brought that chapter to a close, and I got back a little peace of mind. Things looked a little brighter. In point of fact, the story of my imprisonment would not be complete if I didn't share that I was the beneficiary of a small miracle. It occurred during my third week at Holloway.

I could not sleep. Thoughts of Rats and Felix kept me awake, as did the chilliness and dampness of the cell. Forced to sleep with only two blankets as thin as sheets, a chill had taken root in my bones, and I found it impossible to get comfortable. A warder named Marie understood. One night, as I huddled under my blankets in the dark, shivering, I heard the jingle of keys and a soft voice asking if she could come in. "I have something for you," she said. The words were so extraordinary that for a moment I thought I might have misheard them. What does she want with me in the middle of the night? I couldn't see what she was carrying—it was too dark—so I waited, listening to her footsteps, sensing rather than seeing her approach. She dropped something soft and heavy on my cot. A warm body pushed against my stomach. It was a cat, a large tabby cat. I reached out and petted his head, ran my fingers through his fur. It felt silky. Marie said she would allow me to sleep with him—"Caspian" she called him—if I promised not to tell anyone and agreed to let her take him back each morning before she finished her shift. Otherwise there could be trouble.

"Yes, of course, I agree," I said, thinking that I must be dreaming to imagine a warder would take such a risk for me, telling myself that someday, if I ever got out of prison, I'd repay her with a diamond necklace or ruby earrings. Never, not in my entire life, had I received so unexpected and generous a gift. For an instant, Marie—and Caspian—changed the whole character of my imprisonment. The dampness and coldness of my cell vanished; my shivering ended; I felt myself becoming softer, less apprehensive, less brittle.

I later found out that there were several cats that made the prison their home, with the administrators' full approval. It was the only effective way to keep the rodent population in check. Caspian seemed too fat and sluggish to be much of a mouser, but he was a fabulous sleeping companion. He slept on my chest. His loud steady purr calmed me, made me feel less lonely, less foul and unwanted, but best of all, the dear cat generated an astonishing amount of heat.

17

On Monday morning, January 7, 1935, they came for me and drove me to London in a police car. A mob of people filled the street outside the Old Bailey. Some hurled eggs. Somebody even threw a dead cat at me. It seemed to me that no one in England was on my side. Everyone thought of me as a vulgar, selfish, callous woman. Even the weather fitted into the scene: the morning was ice cold and the sky gray with feathery wisps of gray cloud; they kept blowing across darker blacker clouds billowing up from the horizon. God, it was cold that day. But I was not paying attention. As I trudged past the maze of people of all kinds, gesticulating people, shouting people, aggressive and demented people, all trying to get my attention, I touched my hair. Would he think my hair ugly now? Would he think of me as old? Vanity is a word for what I was feeling. As two police-men escorted me through the hubbub in the courthouse cor-ridors, reporters' cameras clicking and flashing, I feared that on seeing me he might realize what a laughable mistake he had made. How could he have selected such a hag as a lover? But other words such as yearning also applied. I yearned to see his face again: his eyes, his lips, smiling at me, speaking to me, mouthing something to me across the courtroom, words like, "chin up" and, "I love you." I imagined myself capable of withstanding anything if he gave me even the smallest sign of affection.

I looked across the courtroom at the other prisoner dock. He was sitting there, his eyes cast down, elbow on the ledge, cheek on his hand, a new shadow on his upper lip. How thin he looked. I felt an impulse to wave and call to him, and then to run to him and fold him in my arms. My darling boy, I thought. And then suddenly I remembered the way his chest looked when his shirt was off, how smooth and hairless. The strange thing is that I knew that I should not look at him. Let the jurors for one moment catch us signaling each other and it was all over. If we signaled at each other, we would look like conspirators. I felt a thousand eyes covering my face, searching for signs of our scheming criminal souls. The important thing was to get out of this alive. "You can't make Felix an orphan," Irene had said. I must remember that. So I lowered my eyes. Once seated, I distracted myself by doodling on my writing pad, and did manage to sketch the judge in his wig and robes, the royal lion and unicorn, although I could not quite stop the trembling in my stomach or my eyes from rising now and then to glance in his direction.

A sudden pounding of the gavel succeeded in quieting the room. Somebody got to his feet.

"Alma Victoria Rattenbury and George Percy Stoner, you are charged with the murder of Francis Mawson Rattenbury on the third of November last. Alma Victoria Rattenbury, are you guilty or not guilty?"

"I plead not guilty."

"George Percy Stoner, are you guilty or not guilty?"

"I plead not guilty."

Mr. R. P. Croom-Johnson, the beaky, grim-jawed senior prosecutor, opened by touching all the familiar bases: dominating woman . . . mere lad . . . guilty passion . . . diabolical plan . . . martyred husband. At first it was absorbing to hear myself talked about in open court, it was such a novel experience, but then Croom-Johnson seemed to go on forever, and by the time he came to the conclusion, his voice had thickened with contempt and I began to feel a definite resentment to hear myself characterized in such a malicious way.

Next came the opening statement for the defense, which I found even more dismaying. There were times when it actually seemed as though Percy's counsel, Joshua Caswell, a short youthful man who might have been nice-looking if he had not been rather fat, was putting more energy into defending me than Percy. Obviously, quite obviously, Percy had ordered him to emphasize my innocence. When he introduced his case to the jury, he told them, "You might find it a little perplexing that the prosecution has put both accused in the dock and said, 'We cannot show you one did it more than the other.' " Was it perplexing because his client didn't deserve to be in the prisoner dock alongside me? No, that wasn't it. Caswell thought it perplexing that I was there. He didn't think I deserved to be tried alongside Percy and recalled the case of another adulterous couple, Bywaters and Thompson, who had been tried at the Old Bailey some years before. They had also been accused of murdering the woman's husband, and both were convicted and hanged. "If you remember that case," he said glancing at his notes and speaking with deliberate slowness, in a voice that always seemed to tremble from forced restraint, "and if you have confused it with this in any way, think again, because in that case there was evidence beyond dispute that the two people before the jury were both there when the fatal blow was struck. You might have read about that case, since many doubts have been expressed as to whether one of those two people was rightly convicted. That is the sort of thing you will be particularly careful to see does not happen here. There must be no mistake. Can you imagine any crime which bears less evidence of having been the result of two people working it out before?" He concluded with a strong sense of theater. His voice rang out.

"My submission to you is that the only explanation of this case is that it was the act of one, and the impulsive act of one, and I might add the mad act of one."

This was *Percy's* counsel?

The remainder of the first day was taken up with the tedious examination and cross-examination of six police officers, the unearthing of the smallest inconsistencies and points of fact. I let my attention wander. I sat sketching a caricature of my vigorous rumpled counsel, with half my mind listening to him cross-examine Inspector Carter, when all of a sudden the proceedings seemed to reach a really absurd level of pettiness, now addressing, among other things, the distinction between the terms "normal" and "quite normal."

"Had you ever seen this woman before in your life?" O'Connor asked.

"Never," said the inspector.

"You were present when she signed her confession at eight-fifteen?"

"Yes."

"And you have told us that she was then normal?"

"I did."

"Did you say she was quite normal?"

"Possibly I did."

"*Was* she quite normal?"

"Yes."

Here O'Connor turned to face the jury, stretching out the moment before delivering his punch-line. Then he turned to his witness, raising his voice in mock stupefaction. "Would you mind telling me how you can judge whether a person you have never seen in your life before was *quite* normal?"

The inspector was looking a little despondent. The courtroom grew hushed. "I do not know," he said.

Then to eliminate any doubt that he knew the exact weakness of every piece of evidence used against me, O'Connor played a similar trick on Detective-Constable Sidney Bright, who had earlier testified that he was as certain as Inspector Carter that I was "quite normal" when I signed my confession.

"Are you sure she was quite normal?" O'Connor asked.

The witness stirred uneasily, sensing that the boom was about to be lowered on him. "Yes, sir."

O'Connor paused to regard the high rococo ceiling. He was going to deliver another punch-line and wanted to be sure everyone heard it. "Would you have let her drive a motor car?"

"Well . . ." the detective-constable answered, taking out his handkerchief, "I don't know."

"Why not, if she was quite normal?"

"I didn't know if she could drive a car," he said, rolling his handkerchief into a ball. "I don't know whether she has ever driven before."

I tried not to laugh; I did smile.

Back in the courtroom the following morning, where a series of character witnesses took turns informing the jury that Percy was a good honest boy, the best boy that you have ever seen in your life, and that I was the sort of woman who comforted her husband, loved her son, and was kind to every stranger who came to her gate, my mind began to wander again. However, Irene's testimony recaptured it. It was good to see her round face again, her round sad cheeks. On stepping into the box, she threw a glance at me, and kept touching the mole at the side of her forehead as she gave evidence.

O'Connor began by asking her to describe my relationship with Rats, trying to establish that Rats and I had a relatively calm, friendly relationship, and that the worst quarrels we ever had were, as he termed it, "just little tupenny-ha'penny affairs." Then he turned to my behavior on the night of the assault. He'd prepared me. He'd explained his strategy: show the Rattenbury woman to be behaving like a wanton floozy on the night of the murder, expose her as a shallow party woman, and the jury has to reject the image of her as a cold, determined, premeditating murderer. It puzzled me at first why what would count as bad behavior in someone could be used to support her claim to innocence, and I really couldn't understand why everyone had to know I was sodden with drink that night and that I tried to kiss one of the inspectors, but then I told myself, I know I'm really not a wanton floozy, so why should it matter if others think I am? I should welcome this image if it contributes to my defense. But, my God, it embarrassed me, her testimony.

"The night of the assault, was she playing the radio-gramophone?"

In a barely audible voice: "Yes."

"Was she dancing?"

"Yes."

"Was she drinking?"

"Yes."

"And did you see her making-up to the police?"

"Yes."

The mention of "making-up" stimulated a distinct ripple of laughter in the courtroom. The reporters' pencils flew across their pads. This was the good stuff. This is what their readers wanted.

Justice Humphrey didn't hesitate. He stared stonily and the laughter quickly died. He was a rather obese man in his mid-sixties whose eyes and brows drooped at the outer corners so that his expression was always one of gentle disapproval.

"Now if you don't mind, was she trying to kiss them?"

"Yes, she was trying to kiss all of them."

There was another ripple of laughter and another stony stare from the judge.

"Did one of the police officers complain to you about her trying to kiss them?"

"He did not complain but he said something about it."

"What did he say?"

"Well, he said he was going to fetch another police officer."

"Do you know why that was?"

"I suppose it was because of Mrs. Rattenbury."

"Because of her trying to kiss him?"

"Yes."

This provoked still more laughter. Everyone seemed to be thoroughly enjoying themselves—everyone except Justice Humphrey who glared and pounded his gavel, and Irene who blurted, frowning, "Well, it wasn't funny. It wasn't at all like that. She was drunk. That was all, and she was very upset—"

She wanted to continue but O'Connor cut her short. "Quite so. That's all right. Thank you very much, Miss Riggs."

She turned and gazed at me. Her hand covered her mouth but I could still see her trembling chin; she looked as if she was at the point of bursting into tears.

It was here the judge called luncheon recess. There was a collective rumble as people rose to their feet and headed to the exits. O'Connor came up to me, rubbing his hands together. He said he thought Irene's testimony went well.

"It went better than I hoped for, actually. The playful, drunken, dancing, and sexed-up woman—we really got that across. I know it was rather uncomfortable for you to hear, but now the jury members have to ask themselves how a woman who'd just murdered her husband in cold blood could behave like a clown. You see what I mean? It's impossible! Believe me, the laughter reinforced that."

And I believed him too. Although it was on the tip of my tongue to say, "You should have thrown a pie at me." I was prickling with anger and for a moment imagined what it would be like to slap him. What kind of insensitive ass had I gotten myself mixed up with, I thought. But I kept my thoughts to myself. He wasn't trying to embarrass me and I never doubted his competence. He was doing what had to be done to get me off the hook. Besides, I wasn't worried about my dignity or pride any longer; I just wanted the ordeal to end. Obviously, I couldn't afford to antagonize my own counsel. With a patronizing squeeze of my shoulder, as if to say, keep it up old girl, you're doing fine, he left me and for some minutes nothing happened. Then Dr. O'Donnell was called to the stand to establish my level of intoxication on the morning I confessed. Seems I was doubly intoxicated from alcohol and morphia. I was surprised to learn that he sent me to bed with an injection of a half-grain of morphia. I had no idea. I glanced at the jury and saw that they were surprised too.

O'Connor was pacing the room with his hands in his pockets, his eyes on the jury, when he asked the physician whether he could form an opinion as to whether I was in a fit condition on Sunday morning at eight-fifteen to sign a murder confession.

"I feel I can form such an opinion," O'Donnell spoke out with an air of professional hauteur. He pulled himself up in his chair.

"And what is that opinion?"

"That taking into consideration the level of morphia I gave her the night before, and that she was dazed when I saw her the next afternoon, it is clear to me that she was not fit to make a statement to the police. Not by any stretch of imagination could I say she was fit to make a statement that would be construed as either valid or reliable."

The curious thing, I thought, upon witnessing this display of medical certainty, was how wrong the doctor was. My statement was neither valid nor reliable, but not because I'd been under the influence of morphia. It was invalid because I was shielding

Percy. My mind, at the time I signed my confession, had been completely lucid.

It was beginning to seem rather remarkable to me that so much of the trial seemed to hinge on how cock-eyed we were, and even more remarkable that Percy's counsel seemed to have nothing beyond Percy's supposed drug use to offer as a possible defense. This became more and more apparent the next morning when five doctors were called to testify on the credibility of Percy's claim to being under the influence of cocaine at the time of the murder. Four said he could not possibly fit the profile of a cocaine addict and one, as I said already, testified that Percy described cocaine as "brown with dark specks on it," which made it seem that he had never even seen the drug.

What made Percy's case appear hopeless, though, was that the one doctor who did think Percy a cocaine addict, a seventy-six-year-old physician by the name of Lionel Weatherby, was quickly revealed to be incompetent. I couldn't believe my ears. In my lifetime, I've had occasion to meet all sorts of physicians but I had never met one like this. His appearance was not particularly out of the ordinary; it might almost have been that of any other gaunt seventy-six-year-old physician except that his nose was unusually prominent and dripping, as if he had just snorted a dab of snuff, and this made him wipe it with a handkerchief each time he spoke. His speech was far more remarkable. There was no means of telling what he would say next, or how any testimony he gave could possibly benefit Percy's case.

Caswell was going over Weatherby's qualifications, asking questions which the doctor answered with a nod of the head, when the judge intervened with a rare show of impatience. "Dr. Weatherby," he said, with a scowl, "would you mind answering with a yes or a no, because the shorthand writer has to take your answer down, and he cannot take down a nod."

"I am very hard of hearing, my lord," replied the doctor. "Would you mind saying that again?"

"If you hear the question," said the judge, raising his voice, "will you be good enough to answer yes or no. Do not just nod. You understand the reason—the shorthand writer has to take down your answer."

"Yes, my lord."

"When you interviewed Stoner in prison," Caswell resumed, "did you notice any physical symptoms of cocainism?"

"Yes."

"What were they?"

"The physical symptoms," answered Weatherby. "I hardly expected to find them so long after the last dose of cocaine."

"I see. And would you tell the jury what physical symptoms you found?"

"A very definite dilation of both of his pupils."

"Did you test that with the light?"

At this moment, the doctor wiped his nose, and it was well that he did so, for otherwise a largish drop of dark fluid would have dripped from it. "I tested it with the ordinary normal light and with electric light," he said.

"With what result?"

"With the result that the pupils did not react at all either to normal light or to electric light."

"Is that consistent or not with the taking of cocaine?"

"Undoubtedly, it is consistent and very important, and it is due to a definite cause."

"And what is that cause?"

"He was a cocaine addict."

"Did you form any conclusion as to how long he had been an addict?"

"I could only form that conclusion from what he told me himself, and he told me fairly, feasibly, and accurately the effects of cocaine."

"Did the description tally with your own experience?"

"I'd have to say that Mr. Stoner described an hallucination of touch I had never heard before."

"You're saying then—what? That it didn't tally with your experience?" Caswell seemed genuinely perplexed.

"Well, he did describe a rash under his skin that he said seemed to move about. And these sorts of hallucinations—hallucinations of sight—I've had ample experience with them. I had a case under my care of a doctor who had a drinking problem. He had the most horrid hallucination of sight. He saw insects crawling over his clothes, over his bedclothes, and it kept him in a terrible state of agitation—"

Caswell could see that his expert witness was floundering, adrift. So he tried to pull him back onto shore with a question that was simple, and could only be answered in one way.

"Tell me, Dr. Weatherby," said Caswell, "is the description of what Stoner did—the sudden attack on his employer with a mallet—is that consistent with his having taken a dose of cocaine or not?"

"No," replied the expert.

Caswell looked flabbergasted. There he was, feeding his star witness a question that could only have one answer if his client was to be found innocent, and his witness didn't give it.

"What?" Caswell said, not believing his ears.

"No," came the answer again.

"Maybe you did not catch my question," said Caswell doing his best to compose himself. "I was asking you whether attacking Mr. Rattenbury with a mallet was consistent with Mr. Stoner having taken a dose of cocaine that evening."

"Yes," said the doctor, "it is consistent."

"Thank you, sir."

The judge wanted more, however. "Is it also consistent with

his not having taken a dose of cocaine, but being very angry and jealous of his mistress?"

"I am not hearing."

The question was repeated, more loudly. The witness hesitated, wiped his nose with his handkerchief, and the judge asked. "Did you hear?"

"Yes."

"Well?"

"I don't understand, my lord. I don't understand the question."

"You don't understand," repeated the judge. "Very well. I'll let it go."

Caswell decided to wrap it up with a general question. It would have been wiser if he had left well enough alone. "Dr. Weatherby, are there any other conditions which, according to you, lead you to believe that Stoner had taken cocaine that day, as he says?"

"I cannot quite catch the question."

"Are there any other medical matters you desire to mention?" offered the judge.

"Any other medical matters?" echoed the doctor.

"Yes," said the judge, "that's what you are here for, you know, as a medical expert."

The medical expert paused to think for a second, not more, and then he suddenly said, "I do not think any more than I have already said."

The judge nodded his head grimly. "No more," he said. "Thank you, sir. That will be all."

"No further questions," O'Connor said.

Thereupon, this medical apparition, this senile old man, was thanked by O'Connor and stepped down from the witness chair; then he bowed gravely to the judge and counsels, and returned to his seat.

Caswell then declined to call Percy to the stand, which seemed stupid to the point of being derelict. Even though Percy would have to be cross-examined if called to the stand, and every discrepancy in his story of cocaine addiction held up to microscopic scrutiny, failure to call him made it seem he had something to hide. Worse still, failure to call him deprived jurors of the opportunity to see with their own eyes what a sweet, gentle boy he was, to see that he is not the murderer type. At that moment I became convinced that Caswell was only going through the motions; I could see he wasn't even trying to build a persuasive defense for Percy.

When I took the witness stand the following morning I could feel my hands and knees trembling. O'Connor did his best to calm me. His tone was gentle and solemn. He nodded his head to each of my answers, his eyes on the wooden floor, like a priest in a confessional. His first series of questions were relatively innocuous. Did I engage Percy as a houseboy or as a chauffeur? Was that in April of last year? Would I describe his living arrangements, his duties, how he got along with everyone, and so on? Only after about twenty minutes did he turn to our romantic involvement. How long before we became intimate? Where did we have our sexual relations, in my room or his? Could I tell the court why I would become sexually involved with a man so much younger than myself, and a servant?

He was asking the question everyone who followed the case wanted me to answer: how could *she* choose *him?* I winced but answered bravely, describing Percy as a good companion, very affable. I said he made me laugh and we felt tender toward each other, and I added that although it was clear to me that most people would condemn our relationship, my husband did not.

O'Connor wanted me to get across the idea that despite being a married woman, I had free rein: every pleasure I wanted, I enjoyed without opposition. Again, he coached me on the strategy. He intended to establish that I had it made: a young ardent lover in my bed every night, an easygoing undemanding husband, all the money I wanted. It was mortifying, of course, this portrayal. I imagined this appearing in the papers the next day, people laughing. But I understood the importance of presenting myself as a woman without a motive to murder, without conflict, a woman who was fully satisfied with her life up to her husband's murder. "If we can show you had no motive, you're free," he had said. This way of presenting my case actually seemed shrewd to me, so that when the prosecution argued I killed Rats to get him "out of the way," my defense could then turn around and ask, What, gentlemen of the jury, was her husband in the way of?

"As I understand it," said O'Connor picking up on the theme of Rats' indulgence, "there was no occasion on which you told your husband about Stoner, but you would say he knew about your relationship?"

"Yes."

"Why do you believe that?"

"Because we live in a very small house. He must have heard our conversations; he saw us together."

"Was your husband in the house when you had relations with Stoner?"

"Yes."

"Where would your husband be at the time?"

"In his study; he always slept there."

"That is immediately below your room?"

"Yes."

He mentioned that I had a reputation for being rather free with money and asked if I'd mind explaining what the financial arrangements were between my husband and myself.

"I had, of course, an account of my own and a checkbook of my own."

"Which we know was often overdrawn?"

"It was always overdrawn for years."

"During the whole of your married life, did your husband ever ask to examine your banking records, to see your checkbook stubs?"

"No."

"Did he ever ask to see your passbook?"

"No, never."

"Had you any money of your own?"

"Yes, from writing music; I wrote songs."

"I do not find any payment into your account from a music publisher?"

"Well, because when I received checks for my music I used to cash them here and there and spent the ready cash at once on the house."

"So your banking account was fed only by checks from your husband, with no questions asked?"

"Yes."

"Which is what you would define, I think, as a cozy arrangement?"

"*I object, my lord!*" Croom-Johnson was on his feet. "This is forcing the witness to draw a conclusion."

"Sustained," the judge said. "The jury will please disregard the counsel's last question. Proceed Mr. O'Connor."

O'Connor had been looking at the judge. Then turned sharply to face me, as if to catch me off guard with his next question.

"Mrs. Rattenbury, would you mind telling the jury whether you and your husband did anything together on this last night; in particular, did you do anything together immediately prior to the attack on him?"

I didn't answer at first because I was actually caught off guard. We hadn't rehearsed this line of questioning, but then O'Connor repeated the question and I thought, if I don't maintain my composure, if I appear to waffle, my entire testimony could be thrown out as spurious.

"We slept together," I said.

The courtroom took in a collective breath. Even the whispering counsels paused to take this in.

"When you say 'slept together' does that mean sexual intercourse?"

"Yes."

"Was that a normal thing for you to do with your husband?"

"No, it was not."

"When was the last time you and he had sexual intercourse prior to that night?"

"About six months ago."

O'Connor nodded soberly, approvingly. "Now, Mrs. Rattenbury," he said, "did Mr. Stoner know you had intercourse with your husband that night, the night of the murder."

"Yes," I said.

He paced in front of me before asking his next question. "How did he know you had intercourse with him?"

"He told me."

"When did he tell you?"

"After the assault on Rats."

"In bed?"

"Yes."

"And you remember quite well what he said to you, and every word that was said to you by Stoner, in bed, right after the assault?"

"Naturally."

"Now if you will, Mrs. Rattenbury, how did Mr. Stoner indicate that he knew you had had intercourse with your husband earlier that night?"

I suddenly felt a chill go through my arms and spread upward toward my shoulders and face with this realization: O'Connor was using my testimony to establish Percy's motive. Now I remembered his instructions. Motive is everything, he said. "If we can show you had no motive, you're free." The same should go for Percy. Isn't motive his whole case? If he had no motive, then killing Rats was an act of insanity. But if he had a motive, he's guilty of murder in the first degree. I saw O'Connor's strategy: Percy who killed Rats in a jealous rage, who had every reason to be in a jealous rage, would absorb all the blame.

I looked away, out the window at the sky, as tears rose to my eyes. Then I let my eyes glance past Percy. He was watching me, not moving.

O'Connor repeated his question. I remained silent. The judge leaned toward me. He spoke in a gentle encouraging voice. "Mrs. Rattenbury, please answer the question. How did Mr. Stoner know you had had intercourse with your husband on that night?"

One tear spilled over and I wiped it away with the back of my hand. "He told me he heard me come out of my husband's room and so assumed that we had."

"I see," the judge said.

"Tell me, please," O'Connor resumed. By this time, the courtroom was so still one could've heard a pin drop. "Did he indicate that he assaulted your husband right after he saw you leave his bedroom?"

"Yes."

"And did he tell you how that knowledge—the knowledge that you had just had intercourse with your husband—did he tell you how it made him feel?"

"Yes."

"What did he say?"

I did not answer.

The judge leaned forward again. I thought a hint of irritation

creased his brow. "Please answer the question, Mrs. Rattenbury."

I felt nearly dizzy. *Mother of God!* How could I have failed to
see this coming? I recognized that if I answered I might be eras-
ing any small chance Percy had to establish his innocence. I
couldn't answer, couldn't sacrifice Percy, couldn't say it. Then
all of a sudden I *did* say it.

"He was jealous." I said it because I had to; because there
was nothing else I could say that would've appeared truthful.

"Was that the word he used—jealous."

"Yes, he said it made him feel jealous."

Percy stretched suddenly and I looked at him. He was faintly
smiling. He glanced at the jury with an air of cool detachment
and then at his counsel, and then looked back at me.

"Three more questions, Mrs. Rattenbury," O'Connor said,
smiling gently. "Did you murder your husband?"

"Oh, no," I said. "Oh, no . . . no."

"Did you take any part whatsoever in planning it?"

"No."

"Did you know a thing about it till Stoner spoke to you in
your bed?"

"I would have prevented it if I had known half—a quarter of
a minute before, naturally."

"Thank you," O'Connor said. "That is all."

It was now Croom-Johnson's turn to cross-examine. He got
slowly to his feet, and looking very grave, very Old Testament,
proceeded to cover the same ground as O'Connor. With two
main differences: he had the nasty habit of pointing his finger at
me as he spoke and he seemed fascinated by our household
sleeping arrangements—fascinated in particular by the fact that
Felix's bedroom was directly across the hall from mine, and
that he slept with his door open. "Are you suggesting to
members of the jury that you, a mother, fond of her little boy of

six, was permitting this man to come into your bedroom with you, across the hall where your innocent child was asleep with his bedroom door open?" I still do not know why my counsel did not object. It was improper and irrelevant, intended only to portray my character in a negative light, as immoral, beneath contempt. But I answered as best I could, truthfully, by saying that I was confident that my sleeping with Percy had no adverse effect on Felix. Even if he had heard voices coming from my bedroom—which is extremely doubtful since he is a very sound sleeper—he wouldn't have been troubled; he got along well with Percy; they were friends.

The last person called was Percy's father. He testified that Percy couldn't have found cocaine in his house because he has never had cocaine, or morphia, or any drug, of any description, in his house.

Caswell declined to cross-examine, "in view of the witness' natural conflict of interest."

Then after a brief recess Caswell stood and made his closing statement, once again focusing on the question of character. He said he might expect a crime like this from a sadist, a man who killed for the pleasure of it, or from a man of hot blood and of Latin race, urged on perhaps by jealousy or some kindred emotion, but not from a boy like Percy, an English lad with a good solid record, a record with not a scratch, not a stain, not a blot, a splendid record. Which made him closely study the explanation suggested by the prosecution—to get Rattenbury out of the way. But he found that unsatisfactory because it led to the same question raised by my counsel, Whose way was Rattenbury in? "There was nothing to keep Stoner from what had been termed adulterous intercourse; everything was ready for him, everything was there." Caswell provided no evidence beyond Dr. Weatherby's "expert" testimony that Percy used cocaine, a fatal omission. Which, nonetheless, did nothing to prevent him from claiming that he had indeed "proven, and inevitably proven, that this young man's crime was an act of impulse, the act of someone who did not plan beforehand, who made no necessary provision for the future, and acted under an impulse, as I suggest to you, an uncontrollable drug-induced impulse."

We were given barely a few moments to recover from this charade before Croom-Johnson stood and again summarized the case for the Crown, speaking with more hostility and poetic license than he had shown at any other time during the trial. "She, gentlemen of the jury, was like a sex-crazed beast, waiting for the opportunity to strike. Not only did she indulge in the most shameful orgies while her child slept only a few feet away, but when her husband was in bed, she and her lover went in and committed this cold-blooded, terrible murder, the most vicious murder that has ever happened in the annals of England or the British Empire." He was scandalized, appalled at the possibility that jurors might not hold us accountable—fully accountable—for our crimes.

He, obviously, had far less intelligence than my own counsel who arose with an air of melancholy, although not a melancholy for his client. His melancholy was for the jurors since they had the supremely difficult task of recognizing the innocence of a woman whom most would be inclined to reproach for moral reasons. My counsel struck me as sophisticated, to the point of being cunning. He dwelled on the nausea and disgust they should feel for me, the way I ensnared and degraded this hapless youth, which was bound to make it harder for them to limit themselves to their duty, which was to answer this question, and this question alone: Is she or is she not guilty of murdering her husband?

I very much liked O'Connor's suggestion of what jurors might do if tempted to condemn me for moral reasons. He would say to them, with reverence, "Let him that is without sin cast the first stone." But most of what he said was said before: Why would I want to get Rats out of my way? Why would I exchange my comfortable luxurious surroundings with my car and villa for life with Percy on a pound a week? If I had the foresight and cunning attributed to me, how could anyone square that with the idea that I sat down with Percy and solemnly decided upon a mallet for the execution of the act? Why a mallet? Doesn't the clumsiness of the crime brand it as an act of impulse?

Only one of his arguments struck me as new, his interpretation of my confession. "The Crown asks you to convict her on the basis of these statements. She says to Bagwell at about three in the morning: 'I know who did it. I did it with a mallet. It is hidden. Rats has lived too long. It's urine on the chair.' A rambling incoherent statement. It is suggested that this is a confession. But if it is a confession, why does it not confess the truth? Why does she not say to the police: 'I will show you where the mallet is?' You will find, as her statements progress throughout the night, there is one strange lacuna. On no occasion does she tell the police where the mallet is hidden. Can you imagine any reason for this omission other than the fact that she did not know?"

O'Connor closed by once again shifting all the blame to Percy. It made sense in terms of establishing my innocence; it was a brilliant strategy in that respect. And the truth is I did not wish to die; I did not wish to be found guilty, but the idea of establishing my innocence by proving Percy's guilt caught me by the throat; it made me nauseous.

"Perhaps the most horrible part of my task in the performance of my duty to Mrs. Rattenbury," O'Connor concluded, "is to have to call your attention to facts which clearly indicate that Stoner conceived and executed the crime. But that duty must be discharged. Stoner, as you know, is still but a lad, but the evidence shows him to have been an unbalanced melodramatic hysterical boy. Consider that this affair was his first association with passionate womanhood. Consider too that he admits to killing his mistress' husband. His learned counsel says he is bewildered by the question of motive. He asks, why would this young man commit murder? Gentlemen of the jury, doesn't the fact that he saw her step out of her husband's bedchamber only moments before the assault satisfy the question of motive? Stoner was jealous; he told her so himself. He murdered his mistress' husband in a jealous rage. I beg you, as I began, to discount your horror at this woman's moral failure and to remember that the worst failure that you could inflict upon this wretched youth would be to convict her of something for which she knows she is not responsible. Mercifully, perhaps you may say to yourselves: 'She has been punished enough. Wherever she walks she will be a figure of shame. She will bear to her grave the brand of reprobation, and men and women will know how she acted.' That is not to say she is to be branded a murderess, that her son is to go down as the son of a murderess; that justice is to be prostituted because you have been misled because of your hatred of the life she has been leading, because of thinking she has done something she has not done."

Then Justice Humphrey gave his instructions to the jury, which made almost no sense to me. Something about how it is not a pleasant thing to have to say anything about my moral character, although he had to grant that my own counsel only a moment before said things about me which must have been very painful for me to hear, if, indeed, I had any moral understanding at all. Still, he felt it necessary that jurors form an opinion of my character, the sort of woman I am, a woman so lost to all sense of decency, so entirely without morals, she would stop at nothing to gain her ends, particularly her sexual gratification.

His condemnation of my character seemed to me interminable. With every word he uttered his brows became droopier, his voice slowly receding, growing flatter and colder with distance. At his conclusion, however, I pricked up my ears. "Members of the jury," he said, "having heard her learned counsel, having regard to the facts of this case, it may be that you will say that you cannot possibly feel any sympathy for that woman; you cannot have any feeling except disgust." But instead of him saying that jurors' disgust for me should make them more certain of my guilt, he said it should make them less certain. After letting this paradox sink in for a moment, he provided the explanation: jurors needed to work conscientiously to compensate for their natural tendency to revile me because I am an adulteress, and an adulteress, he added, "of the most unpleasant type." That is how he disposed of me: by warning jurors to guard against their inclination to convict me. He made quicker work of Percy. In less than five minutes, he wiped out his entire defense.

"As for Stoner and the question of his insanity, I have studied the question and cannot find a shred of evidence to suggest he did not know what he was doing when he committed this crime. Therefore I have to say to you, consider the question settled as to whether this young man was suffering from a defect of reason through disease of mind. My instruction to you, members of the jury, is that so far as the insanity defense is concerned, you are bound to reject it upon my ruling. That is all I desire to say with regard to Stoner."

The jury retired at 2:28. It was nearing four o'clock when they returned with their verdict. Percy and I rose to our feet.

The clerk of the court put the question to the jury: "Gentlemen of the jury, do you find Alma Victoria Rattenbury guilty, or not guilty?"

"Not guilty."

Irene let out the cry of a wounded and suffering beast about to be put out of her misery.

The judge continued. "Gentlemen of the jury, do you find George Percy Stoner guilty or not guilty?"

"Guilty."

At that word, which was spoken softly, light swam before my eyes, and then found shape in his face, which was in profile, turned to the judge. He stood there for a full minute while the judge bowed his head over court records, entering the sentence in a silence so complete that the only sound in the room was the scratching of his pen. He lifted his head and spoke: "I've passed the only sentence which the court knows—death by hanging." Then he asked if Percy had anything to say as to why that sentence should not be passed upon him. "Nothing at all, sir," came the answer. It was the only time, from beginning to end, that he spoke.

I tried to move, to go to him, but my legs were like jelly. It was all I could do to stand. Then he turned his head to me. "Good-bye, Percy," I said; or perhaps I only think I said good-bye. Then the guards directed him toward the stairway to the cells, and he was gone.

18

It was almost dark, an icy snow falling—not in vertical lines, but in a twisting horizontal deluge, the sort that closes shops and schools. The streets were almost empty. O'Connor was driving Irene and me to the house of Keith Miller Jones, Rats' nephew, where she and I were to spend the night. In front of Jones' house, newspapermen crowded in three or four parked cars, smoking and talking. Someone must have sighted me. Car doors opened and men hopped out. They rushed at us. O'Connor pushed down on the accelerator and said, "You can't stay here." A reporter who held a camera aloft ran ahead of the others shouting, "If you go to Bournemouth we'll follow you." I stared at him amazed that he and his colleagues showed so little sympathy just hours after the sentencing. Why were they chasing me? What had I done to them?

O'Connor turned to me after we stopped at the intersection. "Where shall I take you?" he asked. His voice was calm, as though he expected I'd have a ready answer. He gave me a smile.

I didn't smile back. Since I'd heard Percy's sentence, I felt as if everything had darkened, everything had clouded over. I felt as if the whole of my life, in comparison to that moment, had been an April morning. And yet, actually, nothing had become murkier; on the contrary, in that instant of hearing, everything had clarified, only not in the way I wanted.

He waited. Then he said, "I mean, do you want to go to my

house? Or would you rather stay with friends?" Bournemouth was too far to drive, he said, especially in this weather, and even if we made the trip, I wouldn't find any peace there. A crowd, a rather hostile crowd, he was sure, would be waiting. "Or would you rather take rooms in a hotel?"

I nodded. "A hotel," I said.

After a moment, he said he'd take us to the Prince Edward. "You won't be bothered there," he said.

"Good," I answered.

We parked in front of the hotel and Irene and I waited in the car while he secured adjoining rooms for us.

"Are you hungry?" Irene asked.

I shrugged and tried to smile. "No. Not really."

"When do you think you might want supper?"

"I don't know."

She nodded, as though that seemed reasonable.

I was finding her suffocating, which made no sense, because I loved and trusted her. If I trusted anyone, she was that person. It's just that whenever I flinched, whenever I sighed or took a deep breath, so did she, so focused, so concentrated was her attention on me.

"We could have food sent up, you know? We don't have to go out to eat, if that would make you feel more comfortable."

I told her she should eat on her own, without me. If she said another word about food I thought I'd scream.

"Shall I go in and see what's keeping O'Connor?" she said.

"Good idea," I said, resting my head against the back seat and shutting my eyes for a moment. When I opened them again, she was leaning forward, looking out the window at the hotel entrance. "I think I see him," she said.

He was walking down the front steps back to the car. He bent down to tap the window. I opened it, feeling the shock of cold air and snow on my face.

"You can come along now," he said. "I've taken a suite of rooms for you," and we climbed out and he led us into the lobby. "You let me know if you need anything," he said. I thanked him, and he walked back to his car and disappeared into the night.

Upstairs, I shut my door and threw myself down on the bed without a word to Irene. I didn't even stop to take my coat off. Nearly instantly, images of Percy came into focus—one in particular, his turn toward me moments after the judge sentenced him. His smile and smooth brow, his serenity, reminded me of one of those stone Buddhas that decorate the gardens of monasteries and temples. How forgiving his expression had been. The gentlest face, male or female, I had ever seen.

The law only allows one penalty—death—the judge had said. But in O'Connor's opinion, there was a chance for mercy. He had come over to me, smiling, after Percy was taken away. He wanted to congratulate me on the outcome, that I had been acquitted, but when he saw my face, his expression changed. There was a murder and someone had to pay, he told me in a grave voice, his hand squeezing my shoulder. It was either going to be Percy alone or the both of us. Those were the only possible outcomes. It was O'Connor's considered opinion that the decision could have gone the other way if we hadn't been careful. Now we just had to hope they'd grant the boy mercy on account of his age. He'd talk to the prosecution and to Caswell, to see if that was a possibility, and he'd let me know. In the meantime, I had to look on the bright side. His hand was still on my shoulder, squeezing. At least I was free to go home, he said. I could walk away from this. And I said to myself what we both knew, the truth that was too obvious to ignore: *I'm walking away because I testified against him.*

A memory came back—the memory of my recantation. I

tried to think of something else, I tried to recall the time we sang "Dark-Haired Marie" together, how his soft alto voice blended with mine, our voices filling the car, but instead I heard the sound of my own voice: *He came into my bed and told me he assaulted my husband with a mallet. I swear to you he did it on his own, without any encouragement from me. If I had known he intended to hurt Rats I would have stopped him.*

Protecting my son, I called it. Keeping him from becoming an orphan. I knew what that meant now. I had been protecting myself, sacrificing Percy.

I took my coat off and curled under the covers, guilt choking me. Why, oh why, did I have to testify that he saw me come out of Rats' studio? Yes, O'Connor's question took me by surprise, but I suspected he'd ask it. I should have forbidden him . . . or gotten another counsel. I could have. It would have been easy. But something else concerned me more: my survival. I thought I could sacrifice Percy and go on. Even knowing he never would have hurt anyone if not for me, I thought I could go on. And live. And return to my son.

The press is perfectly right about me. I encouraged Percy to kill Rats. I used him, first as a plaything, now as a scapegoat. I actually rejoiced in the failure of his defense. So I can be free to return to my empty, pleasure-seeking, wasteful life.

I remembered how in prison I'd only allowed myself to think of happy times with Percy. I didn't let myself think of his pain, or the likelihood that he'd hang, but now I thought I should hang and no one else.

How much better if I'd been found guilty, if I'd never been released.

Memories continued to surface without order. I saw Percy at my kitchen table again, and remembered how strangely I first reacted to his smile, how uncomfortable his friendliness made me, and I saw him again behind the wheel of our Daimler, his eyes gazing at me through the rearview mirror, his crooked tie, his laughter. After a while, my self-loathing seemed to run out of violence, and I just lay there, looking out the window at the lights in the skyline, each small flicker of light a perfect star. Sometime toward dawn, I fell asleep.

After I opened my eyes, for what seemed the longest time I didn't know who or where I was. Then I saw Irene. How long had she been sitting on the loveseat only a few feet away from my bed?

She asked if I needed anything. She said she could get me a nice cup of tea if I liked, and toast and sausage too. I should eat something. She could stay with me, she said, sit beside me as long as I wanted, said she wouldn't say a word if I didn't want her to.

I didn't need anything, I said.

"Are you sure?" I could hear the disappointment in her voice. "You're probably just exhausted," she said, and then added, "You'll probably feel better tomorrow. You want to see Felix as soon as you can, don't you?"

I shrugged. If only wanting could help. I wasn't sure I could be any use to him. I wasn't sure at all that he was not better off without me. I had always believed he needed me. I didn't believe that anymore.

"I just want to be left alone," I said.

That day and the next and for the next several days, I did not know what to do with myself. I simply could not imagine returning to Bournemouth. The idea of setting foot on the street filled me with terror. I couldn't even imagine getting out of bed. I just wanted to sleep. When I awakened in the morning I'd try to force myself back to sleep, pushing my consciousness back down with the desperation of a drug addict inhaling her last particles of opium. Then, when I could no longer erase consciousness with sleep, I erased it with whiskey.

The day came when Irene refused to purchase liquor for me. She announced that I was killing myself and refused to be a party to it, and then marched back to her own room.

Ten minutes later she opened the door separating our rooms. "You're mistaken, Alma," she said gravely. "You're mistaken if you think everything is over for you. There's so much you could do with your life."

"Oh," I said, "like what?"

"Felix . . . he needs you."

I informed her that I'd given a great deal of thought to Felix and there was nothing in the world I wanted more than to help him grow into a happy, responsible young man. And once upon a time, I thought that I could help him. But now I saw that he doesn't need a mother who is notorious, his father's murderer, the mistress of their chauffeur, the press's leading contender for the title of the most sinful woman in history. How could I make a home for my little boy? How could I play with him, invite other children to join us? Indeed, I had come to the conclusion that if Felix was to be successful and happy in his life, he must try to forget he was even related to me.

She walked toward me, muttering a few words I didn't catch; then when she reached me, she knelt beside me and asked if she could kiss me. No, I said. Then she got back to her feet and touched the gin bottle by my nightstand.

"Do you really need this so very much?"

I made no reply and she continued staring at the gin bottle. Then all of a sudden she turned toward me: "Oh, Alma, I can't hold it back any longer. The trial is over. You're innocent. Don't you understand? *He's* guilty. He killed Rats. Let him pay the penalty." Tears ran down her cheeks. She took my hand. "His guilt releases you."

I told her I didn't want to talk about Percy. But apparently she had more to say on that subject. "I'm just saying that you don't need to destroy yourself, Alma," she said. "You can let go of your guilty feelings. Just give them to Percy; give your guilt to him, darling. He brought this whole mess into being. Let him carry it to the scaffold with him."

I was trying to think of an appropriate response to this. I was trying to find some compassion inside myself, like a closet I could enter, but hearing her refer to the scaffold, something seemed to break inside me, and I said, "And maybe if you hadn't decided to keep me company, maybe I could find a little peace." I said it straightforwardly; I said it slowly. I told her I wanted—*needed*—her to return to Bournemouth now. I told her she was driving me crazy. Then the spirit of self-loathing rising in me (probably also the gin), pushing me to action, sweeping me up as on a flood of intoxication, I went into her room, and I took out her suitcase, and started stuffing her things inside.

This wasn't right, this horrible treatment of her. I said she didn't deserve it. She wasn't to blame, and Percy wasn't to blame either. It's me, I said. I was to blame. I was bad, and I'd always been bad. I was incapable of being any different, and so what? Nothing, nothing mattered anyway.

Then I stumbled toward a chair, dropped into it, slumped without moving.

"Alma," she said kneeling beside me, "you're upset because of all the horrible things that were said at the trial. It was a nightmare. You have to tell yourself that the judge and prosecutor don't know you. They're just arrogant ignorant old men."

"They were right," I said. "They know me better than you do." I tried smiling but she only stared back. Her eyes were glassy, and I noticed that the corners of her mouth were trembling.

"Are you waiting for an apology from me?" I said. "Is that why you're still here? Because if you are, I'm afraid you're going to be disappointed."

"I don't want an apology. I just want to know how in heaven I can help you."

I smoothed my hair down and took a breath. "How you can help me," I said—I could hardly get my breath; all the emotion had left me breathless—"is to leave me alone. That's all I want from you."

She looked at me for a moment, one hand pressed to the side of her forehead.

"That's all I want," I repeated, glaring. "Just that one thing. Would you please do that for me?"

She didn't answer. She just slowly rose to her feet and returned to her room, leaving the door half open. I could see her kneeling in front of her suitcase. When she came out she shrugged, her too-red lips parted, her forehead furrowed, as if not sure what to say. "I'll call tonight to see if you need anything."

I listened to her footsteps go away, then sat down at the desk, thinking I should write letters to Irene and Felix, to apologize for hurting them. But I had no idea what to say. Then I wrote a poem to Percy. And then a moment later tore it up. I felt as though I couldn't even begin to understand what I wanted to say to anyone until I was out of this hotel room. But where should I go? All I knew is I wanted to get out, needed to go somewhere else, and began pacing the suite, looking around frenziedly, as though to find in it something to clarify my thinking, to give me direction. And then I saw it on the desk. I strode across the room and grasped it, the letter opener.

19

It wasn't until I was on the train, my purse between my knees, the letter opener inside, that I finally understood what I was going to do with it. I remember nothing of the journey, except the conductor waking me at Bath.

It was six-thirty. I found a taxi and took it to the hotel. I hesitated once inside the lobby to watch the bellhops and guests, the movement of people, their bright jewels and scarves and furs. For a tense delirious moment, the young man rounding the corner seemed to be Percy; the light was on his back and I couldn't see his face, but he had the same hair and build. "Percy!" I called. But it wasn't him.

I approached the desk. There I asked if I could have the room I occupied last summer, and to my surprise, since the hotel seemed practically full, I discovered it was vacant.

Leaning against the walls for support, I made my way down the hall and into the elevator. I found the room, opened the door, and sat at the foot of the bed I once shared with him. A layer, and then another, of darkness receded, and I could see the French doors, and beyond the doors, the wrought-iron balcony shimmering in moonlight, and below the balcony the city of Bath covered in snow. Then I removed my eyes from the French doors and looked all around the room: all was the way I remembered, the same high ceilings, the same floral wallpaper and curtains of green-and-mulberry brocade, the same tulip-shaped reading lamps. I had a sharp feeling of sadness as I realized that the room was not the same as my last visit.

Percy, of course, was gone.

I rose from the bed, telling myself I was right. My son will be better off. I am protecting him. I am protecting him from the shame of being associated with me. In a few years I will be forgotten and he will have forgotten, and he will be able to live his life the same as any other child. What kind of mother would not want to do that for her child? Has a mother ever loved her child more?

I reached into my purse for the letter opener, pulled it out and then walked through the French doors breathing the night air. There was a smell of frost and pine, the fresh winter smell. I stood for a moment feeling the profound beauty of the city-scape—so different from the view last year during the summer. Then, as I stood there looking at the whirling snow, listening to the wind, it suddenly seemed to me that there was something else missing—not just Percy, and not just the chill I should be feeling standing in the cold, but the absence of tactile sensation altogether.

I turned the sharp point of the letter opener to my belly and pressed. No pain. I pressed again and again, still without a flinch, in the same sort of way, I reflected, as a shaman walks on burning coals or sleeps on a bed of nails. I looked down. There was blood on my dress. I put my hand on my stomach. The blood was warm and sticky. I looked at my red fingers and inserted them into my mouth, and as I did, became aware that tears were flowing from my eyes.

You're crying tears of joy, I said to myself, wondering why I should suddenly feel elated.

Then I heard the sound of laughter and understood.

"Why, hello, Mrs. Rattenbury."

He was sitting on the balcony rail wearing his gray chauffeur suit, his hands gripping the iron bar to steady himself, his thin, meager shoulders slightly leaning forward, in a position that was precarious yet full of grace, his round eyes looking directly into mine, smiling as much as to say, Well, here we are again. I'll bet you never thought you'd see me here. Then he spoke aloud, "Alma, why are you crying? Aren't you happy to see me?"

"I'm so sorry, Percy," I said, or tried to say, not only to apologize for my tears, but for everything I'd done to him.

"There's nothing to apologize for." He shook his head, still smiling. "But I would like you to explain to me what you're doing with *that?*" He pointed to the letter opener. "My God! I mean, really Alma."

Until this moment I had not thought about the absurdity of trying to kill myself with a letter opener. I remembered him telling me his mother needed three attempts before killing herself with a shotgun, pulling the trigger with her toe, and I thought about saying, Percy, am I still reminding you of your mother, but I didn't. I didn't say anything. I didn't respond at all. Strength seeping out of me, my mind becoming beautifully still and thoughtless, I just gave thanks to God for making my last moment so simple, so easy, and let go.

ACKNOWLEDGMENTS

For their invaluable ideas and feedback on the manuscript, I would like to thank Brittiany Koren, Carol Severino, Margaret Thompson, Mary Trachsel, and Beth Vesel. Thanks also to the George Eastman House for permission to reproduce Julia Margaret Cameron's Beatrice on the cover.

ABOUT THE AUTHOR

Leslie Margolin is a professor at the University of Iowa with appointments in Counseling and POROI (Project on Rhetoric of Inquiry). He's published four previous books, two academic (*Goodness Personified: The Emergence of Gifted Children* and *Under the Cover of Kindness: The Invention of Social Work*) and two popular (*Murderess! The Chilling True Story of the Most Infamous Woman Ever Electrocuted* and *Damaged*).